D1025048

A Little Bit of Spectacular

GIN PHILLIPS

DIAL BOOKS FOR YOUNG READERS
An imprint of Penguin Group (USA) LLC

DIAL BOOKS FOR YOUNG READERS
Published by the Penguin Group
Penguin Group (USA) LLC
375 Hudson Street
New York, New York 10014

USA | Canada | UK | Ireland | Australia | New Zealand | India | South Africa | China
penguin.com
A Penguin Random House Company

Text copyright © 2015 by Gin Phillips

Library of Congress Cataloging-in-Publication Data

Phillips, Gin.
A little bit of spectacular / by Gin Phillips.
pages cm
Summary: When eleven-year-old Olivia finds a strange message written on
the bathroom walls of a few public places in her new hometown, she finds herself in the midst
of a mystery to solve—and in need of a new friend to help her solve it.
ISBN 978-0-8037-3837-9 (hardcover)
[1. Mystery and detective stories. 2. Moving, Household—Fiction.
3. Friendship—Fiction. 4. Birmingham (Ala.)—Fiction.] I. Title.
PZ7.P535Li 2015
[Fic]—dc23
2013049146

Manufactured in USA on acid-free paper

1 3 5 7 9 10 8 6 4 2

Designed by Jasmin Rubero
Text set in Minister Std

To my grandfather, Thurman Awbrey Kirby.
He made my childhood magical and taught me
to love words.
He also built a pen for my frogs.

A Little Bit of Spectacular

Chapter 1

THE WRITING ON THE WALL

If I were to tell you that three years ago I went searching for a secret, solved a mystery, and changed my life, you might have a few pictures pop into your head. You might imagine me making my way through a dark cave with the glitter of something shiny far ahead. You might picture me fitting a key into an old lock or creeping through the halls of a creaky house with flickering candles.

My guess is that you would not picture me in a bathroom.

I mean, not that you should *start* picturing me in a bathroom.

The bathroom—which you should not be picturing me in—is on 20th Street North in Birmingham, Alabama, at a pizza place called Trattoria Centrale. I went there for the scones, which were delicious, but I also liked to take my time in the bathroom. It was unisex, with one room and one toilet, and the white walls were covered in writing—all different colors and all different handwriting. There were hundreds or thousands of messages from people I'd never met. Or maybe I had. Maybe I'd sat next to the girl in class who wrote "Anything you can do I can do better," or maybe I'd smiled at the guy who wrote "The sky is purple" as I passed him on the sidewalk.

I'd never know—that was the beauty of it. The same sentence that would be boring or silly coming out of someone's mouth was somehow fascinating when it was left behind on a wall.

I had plenty of time to spend reading walls in those days. I'd been in Birmingham less than a month, and once school was out in the afternoon, I didn't have much to do. I didn't know anyone, Gram was at work, and Mom wasn't allowed to leave her bed yet. So I killed time at Trattoria. I had a routine: I placed my order, then I went to the bathroom, and after I washed my hands, I took a few minutes to read the walls. I always found new comments I hadn't noticed before.

This particular day, as I wadded up my paper towel

and tossed it in the garbage, I studied the wall to the right of the doorway. There was a very nice drawing of a red and black rose, a cartoon drawing of a bunny with fangs, and the usual hodgepodge of random thoughts:

Leaving Birmingham for Boise tonight!

I love Audrey Alice Gkrumpke,

and I am going to marry her in August.

You are beautiful.

SOME PIG.

HOT GIRLS READ.

Then, in purple writing, another message caught my eye:

We are Plantagenet. We are chosen.

Well, that seemed odd. The phrasing was odd, I mean. Not "We are Plantagenets," like it was a family name, like "We are Smiths" or "We are Joneses." You could tell people thought it was cool to write odd things on the wall—one of my favorites, "*Marigolds need leashes*," didn't exactly make a lot of sense. But this one seemed weirder than usual. I shrugged and tugged at the door handle.

My cherry rosemary scone was ready, and I picked it up from the counter along with my ice water. The pigtailed lady at the cash register smiled at me. She took my order most days. I probably talked to her more than anyone else in Birmingham other than Mom and Gram.

"Homework?" she asked.

I smiled, but when I tried to answer her, the words wouldn't come out. That was a new problem since I moved here—when people talked to me, sometimes I couldn't talk back. I froze. My mind went blank. It was really inconvenient.

It took a few seconds, but finally I came up with a response.

"Not much," I said. "A few note cards for English."

I was determined to call them note cards. My teacher always called them "conversation cards."

"Tomorrow's chocolate orange," the cashier said, nodding at the nearly empty scone basket. "Your favorite."

If I were a touchy-feely sort of person, I might have felt a little emotional that she knew my favorite scone. That in the middle of this city where half the time my teachers didn't seem to remember my name and where even my grandmother couldn't remember that I don't like butter on my toast, this friendly woman with jet-black nails had noticed what I liked to eat. I might have actually felt my eyes tear up, if I was prone to that sort of thing. But probably I was allergic to pollen.

I settled into a back table and pinched off bites one at a time, chewing slowly to make the scone last longer. If I'd been back home in Charleston, I would have been in one of my favorite bakeries ordering a key lime doughnut or a pumpkin scone and a large vanilla latte. (Mom never had any problem with me drinking coffee. She's always believed coffee is good for the brain.) If it was a bad day and I needed extra comforting, I might have gotten two doughnuts.

Mom believed in enjoying your snacks. But in Birmingham, Gram gave me two dollars a day for snacks and told me to learn to budget. She said Mom and I needed to stop spending money on unnecessary things. So I'd learned to stick to one scone and just get a cup of water.

Eventually I finished up my homework and decided it was probably time to walk home. Gram usually got home a little after five, and she worried if she had to wait too long before I showed up.

"You don't have to rush off," said the lady at the counter. "You're nice company."

Again, my brain was on a five-second delay, which happened even with small talk. Especially with small talk. It was like shyness was a disease, and I'd caught it as soon as I set foot in this city.

"Thanks," I managed finally, when I was already half out the door. "My grandma will worry if I don't get home soon."

Worry drifted around Gram's place those days like nasty-smelling air freshener. Other than that, it was the kind of place where most people would be thrilled to live, even though it wasn't where you would expect to find a little old white-haired grandmother. Gram didn't live in a tidy white house with a big porch and lots of quilts lying around. She lived in a condo downtown, which she'd bought back when she said she wouldn't even take the dog for a walk after dark, and she'd gotten a really good deal on it. You could see all the city lights from her balcony. She didn't have a single inch of carpet—everything was all smooth, shiny hardwood floors and stainless-steel appliances and black stone counters. ("Granite counters," Gram corrected me when I first mentioned them.) Gram loved a nice kitchen.

When I walked through the front door, Gram stood by the gleaming counters chopping lettuce. She still wore her light blue uniform from the hospital where she'd worked forever.

"Any news?" she asked, kissing me on the cheek. "Any tests today? New assignments?"

"Just normal busy work," I said. "I finished everything already."

"Good girl. Your mother's awake."

"She have an okay day?" I asked.

"She's just a little groggy," she said.

"I'll go say hello."

That's about as long as any of my conversations lasted with Gram. Mom said we were still getting used to each other.

The door was open to Mom's room, and I stepped in quietly, just in case she was asleep. Her room had been the guest room until we showed up a few days before Mom's surgery was scheduled. My room used to be Gram's "junk room" and now had my twin bed crammed in with an ironing board, a sewing machine, and an old treadmill.

Anyway, Mom's room was what Gram called "calming," which meant it had no color to it at all—just whites and browns and beiges. The walls were beige and the comforter was beige and Mom's face was beige. No makeup, even though this was the woman who always carried at least a dozen lipsticks in her purse. When I was little she used to let me pick out her eye shadow for the day from a tray of at least fifty colored circles, and even if I picked electric blue that looked like crushed-up Smurfs, she would still wear it.

No color to her now. Just pale skin and tired eyes.

Her eyes were open, and she smiled at me.

"Hey, Mario," she said.

I should mention that my name is not Mario. It's
Olivia. But when I was a baby, I was a super-fast crawler,
like leave-skid-marks-under-my-knees kind of fast.
Apparently Mario Andretti was a race-car driver who
was also very fast. Mom's called me that for as long as
I can remember.

I sat on the edge of the bed, my hip barely touching
her arm. "How you feeling?"

"Awesome," she said, half smiling. "But please don't
make me talk about how I feel. Or how my day was.
Very dull. Tell me something interesting. Tell me, um,
one thing you learned in school today."

"Louise Cormack is offering kissing lessons in the
girls' bathroom after music class tomorrow."

She raised an eyebrow. "That's not exactly what I
meant. And stay away from Louise Cormack."

I grinned. I knew she didn't want to know about
Louise Cormack. Mom and I always loved trivia. *The
Complete and Astonishing Book of World Record Hold-
ers*, *Mysteries of the Strange and Unexplained*, *Weird
and Interesting Facts*—those were my favorite three
books. And even for the weirdest trivia questions,

Mom's answers were usually amazingly close to right.

"Okay," I said, and I thought about a word problem our math teacher gave us. "How much television does the average American teenager watch in a week?"

"Eighteen hours," she said without even pausing. "Maybe twenty."

"Twenty," I said. "How do you know?"

"I have a very impressive brain."

I felt my shoulders relax more than they had all day. This was normal. This was the way things had always been, me sitting next to Mom, shaking my head at her talent for random and pointless facts.

Mom ran a hand through her hair, which I suspected hadn't been brushed all day. "Gram giving you any grief?" she asked.

"Nah. She just wants to know if I got any grades back on tests."

"Make her proud," she said, half smiling again. "Somebody should."

I didn't return her smile because I thought I knew what she meant, even though we'd never talked about it. I got the feeling that maybe Gram was disappointed in Mom. Mom never finished college, even though Gram had worked and worked ("never a holiday, never a day off" she'd say) so that Mom would be the first person in the family to graduate. Mom says college wasn't her thing. The whole time I've been alive, she's worked at a zillion different jobs, mostly through an agency that places her as a part-time secretary. The thing is that when you work part time, you don't get benefits. That means you don't have insurance to pay for doctor bills.

Anyway, insurance and doctors and hospital bills are why we wound up moving here.

Mom hooked one finger through a piece of my hair, twirling it to get my attention.

"You miss home?" she asked, like she was reading my mind.

"I'm okay," I said.

"I know you're okay," she said. "But I also know you miss it. It's okay to say that you miss it. I miss it."

I didn't want to say anything about home. If I said I missed it, if I tried just those three words, all sorts of other words might come tumbling out. It was easier to say nothing.

She breathed in and out, in and out, and I just listened to her. The sound was comforting.

"Did you know," I said, "that puppies are born deaf and blind?"

She just patted my hand and closed her eyes.

"I'm sorry we had to leave, Mario," she said.

When I walked back to the den, Gram was reading the newspaper, and she looked up when I plopped down on the sofa. She pointed to a story on the front page—there'd been a man found unconscious on the sidewalk just a few blocks from the condo. He'd been hit over the head. When the police came, they realized he was wanted for armed robbery.

"It's dangerous for you to walk around by yourself out there," Gram said. "You spend too much time alone."

"Gram," I whined. "I'm walking around in the middle of the day. On crowded streets. It's totally safe."

"Still," she said. "By the way, one of the ladies I work with has a daughter in your grade. Her name is Amelia Glasgow. Do you know her?"

"No," I said.

"She's in a different homeroom from you. But I thought I could set up a playdate for the two of you."

I winced. I'm Gram's only grandchild, and she's always been a little confused about the difference in, say, a three-year-old and an eleven-year-old. Last year, on my tenth birthday, she sent me a pack of Spider-Man pencils and a sippy cup. A sippy cup.

"We don't really call them playdates anymore," I said.

She shrugged and folded the newspaper in half. "You need friends."

"I have friends," I said. "In Charleston."

"You need friends here. And you'd have them if you'd just let them get to know you."

"I have friends," I repeated.

"Waitresses at your favorite restaurants don't count," she said.

She's a cashier, I thought, but it didn't seem worth saying.

Chapter 2

THE WRITING IN THE STALL

The next morning I slid into my desk, pretending to sort through the papers in my folder. That gave me something to look at while the girls in the desks around me chatted with one another. I heard someone say that Mica Norris's mother got a speeding ticket for going 80 miles per hour and somebody else said it was 120 miles per hour. I set a pencil and a pen neatly on my desk. I made sure the pen cap was on very tightly. Someone else said she had eaten octopus the night before and somebody else said gross, and a third person said octopus tasted like chicken.

I slid a piece of paper into my binder pocket. My least-favorite time in school was those few minutes sitting at my desk before the bell rang. It took a lot of effort to look busy.

They talked about sushi for a while. Then someone said that if everyone in China jumped at the same time, the world would spin off its axis.

That's crazy, I thought.

"That's crazy," said Rachel Brock, who sat right behind me.

At least one of them isn't an idiot, I thought.

I heard a pencil hit the floor and roll. When I looked down, I saw a yellow mechanical Bic right by my foot. I reached down and picked it up, turning in my seat toward Rachel. She was dark haired with freckles, and she was one of those people who looks cute with freckles. They were scattered just the right way across her nose and cheeks.

"Is this yours?" I asked.

She nodded and held out her hand.

"Thanks," she said, and she smiled. She smiled at me like you smile at the guy who bags your groceries—nice and polite and distant.

I turned back around. I couldn't come up with any more words. I wasn't even sure I wanted to come up with more words. These girls' conversations weren't all that interesting.

And I was never included in them anyway.

Rachel and her friends weren't like the horrible girls in the movies—they didn't play mean jokes on me or make up insulting nicknames. They just weren't friends with me. Which made sense, I mean, I'd hardly said ten words to any of them. A month ago they didn't even know who I was.

Making friends had never been a problem in Charleston. I didn't need to make them—I'd known everyone forever. I'd met my best friends, Malaka and Evon, in second grade. I still got to call them once a week, but talking was different on the phone. There were weird pauses that were never there when we were face-to-face.

The thought of their faces made me smile. I made fun of Evon for doodling all the time, and I made fun of Malaka for being scared of babies. They made fun of me for being way too neat. They used to pull clothes out of the drawer in my old bedroom and toss them on the floor, then see how long I could stand it before I picked them up, folded them, and put them back in the right drawer.

"One, two, three, four . . . four seconds!" Evon would squeal at me. "You couldn't make it past four seconds? Malaka, throw the skirt!"

Now I sat at my desk and clicked and unclicked my binder ring. As I straightened my already tidy notebook I wondered what if—what if—these girls sitting behind me were perfectly nice and interesting? What if they were really funny like Evon and really smart like Malaka? What if they would like to get to know me, but, like Gram said, the problem was that I wouldn't let them?

Still, how was I supposed to let them get to know me? Just stand up and start telling them my favorite color (purple) and my first pet (a guinea pig) and my most embarrassing moment (the time when I was five and forgot to put on underwear before I went to church and then did a cartwheel in the parking lot and was scarred for life because practically the whole choir saw me)?

That was not going to happen. I did not tell stories involving my underwear.

I put my head down on my desk and wished for the bell to ring. It's sort of interesting how the world changes when you close your eyes—you can hear all sorts of things you didn't notice before. I could hear running footsteps and laughing in the hallway. I heard Rachel banging the heels of her sandals together, and someone across the room dropped their backpack with a thud. I felt the cold hard plastic of the desk against my cheek and I smelled a whiff of chewing gum and erasers.

It was all sort of cozy. Then I felt a tap on my shoulder. My first thought was that Rachel wanted to start a conversation. Not that I was hoping for her to talk to me or anything.

Instead I looked up into the pleasant, wide face of my teacher, Mrs. Snellhawk. She had a mole the size of Brazil on her right cheek. I know that's rude to mention, but it was very hard to ignore because this was the other thing about Mrs. Snellhawk: She liked to get right up in your face when she talked to you.

"Is everything okay, Olivia?" she asked, and I could actually feel her breath on my face. I suspected she'd had orange juice for breakfast.

"Fine," I said.

"Are you feeling sick?"

I had a strong suspicion that my grandmother had told my teachers about Mom. They all had been very nice to me. Too nice. Too *concerned*.

"No, ma'am," I said. "I'm fine."

"If there's anything you need to talk about, you know I'm right here," she said. "Before school or after. We can chat, just hang out a little."

I never liked it when adults said "hang out." And I did not want to chat with Mrs. Snellhawk. She looked at me like she really expected me to open up and share my darkest secrets with her (for example, pantyless cartwheels). I gave up trying to be polite and let myself stare at her mole, which was soft and textured and a little bit like the surface of some far-away planet. I imagined tiny astronauts planting a flag in the middle of Mrs. Snellhawk's mole.

She kept looking at me, all kind-eyed like a deer. I had trouble keeping the image of the tiny astronauts in focus, and instead I thought of Mom's narrow feet peeking out from under her sheets. I blinked.

"May I go to the restroom?" I asked.

She seemed disappointed, but she let me go.

When I got to the bathroom, I washed my hands, even though they weren't dirty. I heard the stupid bell finally ring. I considered myself in the bathroom mirror, wondering if you're born with moles or if they can spring up with no warning. Or if they're like pimples and you can put some cream on them or squeeze them the right way and make them go away. I guessed Mrs. Snellhawk would have tried that already.

I ran a hand over my hair. It's a nice enough dark brown, but it's also big and curly. I've made my peace with it. I don't even try to argue with it anymore—it does what it wants, and I do what I want, and we just agree to disagree. I have no freckles (or moles). Mom once told me my skin was the color of a vanilla latte, which I took as a huge compliment.

I heard footsteps and heard the door start to open. I had this sudden panic attack that it was going to be

Mrs. Snellhawk coming to chat with me, and I darted into the nearest open stall.

Pretty soon I realized it wasn't Mrs. Snellhawk—it was a couple of girls whose voices I didn't recognize. I didn't want to make conversation with them, either, so I thought I'd stay still and give them a few seconds to close themselves in their stalls. I waited. I stared at the toilet paper holder, which was barely attached to the wall by two loose screws. I reached for one screw, wondering if I could twist it back into the wall. I didn't even bother to look at the walls—the school bathrooms were never anywhere near as interesting as Trattoria. Really, if I judged the student body based on what they wrote on the walls, I'd have sworn no one had a creative bone in their bodies. Not even a creative toenail or a creative arm hair. That was why I was entertaining myself with the toilet paper holder. But as I was working a fingernail into the wiggly screw, I noticed one line of tiny handwriting in the middle of all the boring stuff, and I knew it had not been there the last time I looked.

I squinted.

Neatly written in what looked like purple Sharpie, it read:

We are Plantagenet. We are chosen.

And below it, there was another line:

We will never grow old.

I stared. My mouth went dry, and I swallowed. I thought it looked like the same handwriting I'd seen in the bathroom of Trattoria Centrale. I pictured a blurry figure, a man, probably, a man in a trench coat and a hat. Possibly with a cane. That's the kind of person who left clues to be solved. A man hunched over in the bathroom stall, looking both ways, writing his secret message as fast as he could, desperate to escape before he got caught. Desperate for someone to see the message and solve the clue.

Why would he be desperate? Why this particular sentence? And why—here is where my whole fantasy started to fall apart—would a man in a trench coat be writing anything in the girls' bathroom of a middle school?

Okay, so it probably wasn't a mysterious man. There probably wasn't a trench coat. But something was going on.

I stared at the writing a bit longer. It was neat and loopy, kind of elegant. It looked like the handwriting examples on those work sheets you got when you were first learning to write in cursive. It looked like a teacher's writing. It was too perfect.

I waited until the other girls left, then I started working my way down the line of stalls. There were six total, so I started at the one closest to the door and scanned from the top of each wall to the bottom. All I saw were the usual collection of phone numbers and I-love-blah-blah-blahs and the reminders that somebody was here. (Julia wuz here, Everley was here, Jason was here—wait, huh? Hello, *girls'* bathroom. I made a mental note to be very suspicious of anyone at school named Jason.)

No other mention of Plantagenet. No other weird messages at all, unless you counted "Marty Webster has been Bieberized."

I considered the facts: I had read the same highly unusual message in two different bathrooms. It could have been a coincidence. It was probably a coincidence—maybe some girl at my school also hung out at Trattoria Centrale. And that girl was . . . oh, extremely proud to be working at a new store called Plantagenet. A new store that sold antiwrinkle creams. And the girl had super-neat, too-beautiful handwriting like no kid I'd ever met. That was possible.

But as I stood there looking at the lime-colored bathroom walls, the white tiles, and the sinks with big flower-shaped rust stains, I realized that I really, really hoped those words were more than a coincidence. I wanted them to mean something. I spent most of my time feeling like I hardly knew anyone or anything in this city. I wanted to know something. I wanted to have discovered something.

I wanted to be chosen.

I headed back to class before anyone could come looking for me. As I walked through the door, I paused for a split second before I turned and headed to my desk. I glanced at Rachel and her friends, who all looked up briefly when I appeared at the door, then looked back to Mrs. Snellhawk when they realized it was just me. From the corner of my eye I saw Mrs. Snellhawk at the board, drawing some kind of graph. The only sound was the marker on the Dry Erase Board.

I remembered all the times back home when Malaka and Evon and I started laughing at something stupid. We were bad about getting the giggles in class. And I always got in trouble for talking. My grades were good, but my teachers used phrases like "a little too social" and "a bit of a chatterbox," or, if they were really nice, "good with words."

I plunked into my seat without even a whisper of sound. I would make A's in conduct here for sure. I watched the graph taking shape on the board, and as the lines rose and fell, I saw Rachel ease her sandal partly off and dangle it from her toes. Evon used to do the same thing when she was bored in class.

Mom used to do it, too, when she was wearing high heels and they got too tight at the toes. I couldn't remember the last time I'd seen her wear anything but bedroom slippers.

We are Plantagenet. We are chosen. We will never grow old.

Of all the things I could think about, Plantagenet was by far the most pleasant.

Chapter 3

ALIENS AND ARSON

When I got home after school, I stuck my head in Mom's room and saw that her eyes were closed, then I headed straight to Gram's computer, which was about a hundred years old. It took forever to power up. When it finally did, I got online and typed "Plantagenet" as my search term.

If this whole message thing was just some advertisement for a new store in town, I'd find out soon enough.

In a split second, I had 9,250,000 results. That seemed either really good or really bad. I scanned through the first couple of pages and found no references to Plantagenet and Birmingham at all. The first result was about a line of kings who ruled England for over three hundred years, from the 1100s to the 1400s.

King Henrys and King Richards and such—lots of battles and marriages and pieces of land. I read:

> Plantagenet (Plan-ta-juh-nut) was the family name of the ruling house of England from 1154 to 1485. The line started with King Henry II and ended with King Richard III. The Plantagenet reign covered fourteen kings and 331 years.
>
> The Plantagenet line originated when Geoffrey, count of Anjou, married the Empress Matilda, the daughter of Henry I. The term "Plantagenet" was originally derived from the Old English word for plant. There is some thought that the name came from Count Geoffrey's habit of wearing a sprig in his hat or of planting greenery to provide better cover for hunting.

I got a little caught up reading about how one of the Plantagenet families supposedly had demons for ancestors, but I caught myself and got back on track. I didn't see what kings had to do with bathrooms.

There was an Australian winery named Plantagenet and a county in Australia with the same name. There was a Plantagenet medieval archery and combat society in England, which sounded cool, but not really relevant. I came across another society, this one for people who were actually descended from those kings who used to rule England. The website explained that if you were "lineally descended from one or more of the Plantagenet kings" you were encouraged to apply for membership.

Geez. Talk about a snobby club.

There was a Plantagenet type font, a Plantagenet marketing firm (also in Australia), a Plantagenet dog breeding farm, a Plantagenet brand of fertilizer. As I scrolled down farther, the word "aliens" caught my eye. I clicked on the link.

A dancing line of little green aliens bobbed across the top of the screen as I read:

ARE THERE ALIENS AMONG US?
Have You Ever Felt As If You Were Being Watched by Eyes That Were Not Quite Human? It's Not Your Imagination.

The basic tenets of alien-conspiracy theory are well known—strange lights in the sky, flying discs, electrical disturbances, people abducted against their will and used as test subjects for horrifying experiments.

These notions are blatantly ridiculous. Laughable. These so-called UFOs are figments of overactive imaginations. The true story of alien invasion is much simpler. On February 3, 1832, a ship from the planet Plantagenet crash-landed on Earth in a suburb of Chicago. The ship was not disc-shaped—

it most closely resembled a flowerpot. The Plantagenets were not ruthless invaders—they were stranded victims with no way to return to their home world.

Our alien visitors look very much like humans, but they are recognizable by their cerulean eyes and silver hair. They have four hearts and three ears, but the third ear is typically hidden underneath their large hairstyles.

Since the nineteenth century, they have lived among us with nothing but benevolent intentions. The Plantagenets want to help humanity. In fact, they have been responsible for some of the greatest technological advancements: television, airplanes, cell phones, vibrating massage chairs.

Well-known Plantagenets: Albert Einstein, Mark Twain, Betty White, and Anderson Cooper....

I stopped reading, even though I was interested. I had to look up "cerulean," which, it turned out, meant "blue." That was a little disappointing, because I'd hoped the aliens had laser eyes or glowing eyes or maybe eyes growing on tentacles, but, apparently, they just had blue eyes. Still, the idea of aliens communicating through bathroom stalls was sort of cool. Unexpected.

But not very believable.

It was so hard to stay focused when there were hundreds of different directions I could go.

Finally, on the sixth or seventh page of results, I saw "Birmingham" in a sentence involving Plantagenet. The link took me to an old article from the *Birmingham News*.

Local High School Burns to the Ground

January 20, 1995

BIRMINGHAM, Alabama—Bradford T. Plantagenet High School burned to the ground last night after firefighters fought for hours to contain the blaze. Police suspect arson, though no arrests have been made.

The high school had stood vacant for the last seven years since it closed due to structural issues in 1988. Plans to renovate and reopen the school never materialized, despite occasional proposals from the city school board. Police Chief Lisa Woodard said that it's likely a vagrant started the fire, trying to keep warm. Preliminary reports suggest the fire started in the first floor bathrooms.

Built in 1935, Plantagenet High School was known for its high ceilings, polished wood floors, and luxurious library. The high school remained an architectural gem for its first decades, though dwindling funds, roofing problems, and a lack of repairs led to it eventually being condemned.

Next to the article, there was a black-and-white photo of the school with lots of old cars parked in front of it. The building was three stories tall with towers at each side, plus arched windows and even a few gargoyles along the roof. It looked like a castle and a school got married and had this building for a baby.

I reread the article once more and closed the computer. It wasn't as exciting as aliens or secret societies, but it made the most sense. The article was from nearly twenty years earlier—a lot could have changed since then. If this Plantagenet High School had been rebuilt and reopened, the signs in the bathroom would make some sort of sense. Just a girl from some rival school hanging out in our bathroom, maybe? "We Are Plantagenet" did sound a little like a school cheer. As much as I'd rather the explanation be less boring, I had to admit that was more likely than dead kings or aliens with extra ears. I kept scrolling and clicking for a while, looking for any sign of plans to reopen the high school. But I couldn't find anything.

All of a sudden it occurred to me that I had a resource even better than Google right here in the apartment—Mom had grown up here, and she knew everything about everything. She surely knew something about this old school.

I checked Mom's room again and saw she was sitting up.

"Hey, Mom, have you ever heard of Plantagenet

High School?" I asked as I walked into her room.

She turned toward me. I wondered if she'd taken some pain meds recently—her gaze didn't look quite focused. I counted the days in my head—it had been almost two weeks since her surgery. Should she still be taking meds? Should she still be in pain? She said she walked around the apartment like the doctor told her she should, but every time I came home, she was lying in bed. Should she still be there? Should she still be so tired?

I didn't know. I just knew I didn't *want* her to be in bed anymore. I had a flash of a memory of Mom diving into the pool at the Y in Charleston. She's always loved pools more than I do. When we'd go to splash around during the hottest days of summer, all the other moms would sit in lounge chairs and work on their tans, but my mom would be racing me from one end of the pool to the other. She loved to dive, and I could see her toes curled along the edge of the concrete, her arms curved toward the water, her whole body tensed and strong and ready to slide in with hardly a ripple.

It had been four months since I'd seen Mom look strong. That was when she started feeling tired. Then there was a whole bunch of other stuff—passing out, throwing up, bleeding—that came after the tiredness, and eventually the doctors found the tumors, which are the real reason we moved to Birmingham.

Mom found out that the doctors would have to remove the tumors and the parts the tumors were attached to, and she'd need six weeks to recover. At least. No climbing the stairs in our building, no lugging piles of books around at work. It's strange how it takes one little ring of the phone and a voice that says, "This is Meghan from Dr. Ledbetter's office . . . can I speak to your mother?" and life as you know it falls out from under you.

We were behind in the rent already because Mom had been so sick she couldn't work. She said we needed help. So she called Gram, and there was a long conversation I couldn't hear very well, and then we were packing up the apartment and renting a U-Haul truck and then we were here.

She smiled at me from her bed, her arms limp at her sides.

"Plantagenet isn't too far from here," she said. "I mean, it wasn't far from here. It was right at the on-ramp for I-20."

"Have you heard if it's going to reopen?"

"Oh, I can't imagine that it would. There's not much more than a foundation there now. I drove past it a few years ago and it was all overgrown and awful looking. I don't know why the city doesn't bulldoze it and start from scratch."

She scooted over and made room for me next to her. I sank into the mattress, not sure whether to be disappointed or relieved. I'd thought I might have solved the mystery. But if I had, where would that leave me? Back to having scones as the highlight of my day.

"What makes you ask?" asked Mom.

"Nothing," I said. "Just wondering."

I toyed with the sheets, smoothing them over my left leg. I shifted and noticed a bit of red by Mom's arm. I looked closer and saw it was a tiny splotch of blood. Smaller than a dime.

"You're bleeding again," I said.

Mom looked down. She licked her lips and rubbed a hand over her eyes. Eyes that seemed a little swollen.

"It's nothing, Mario," she said. "It's normal. The doctors said there could be a little bleeding while I healed."

I couldn't look away from the red splotch.

"I'm fine, honey." She flipped the sheet over the bloodstain and patted my knee. "I am going to be totally fine. I keep telling you—there's nothing for you to worry about."

"I know," I said, which is what I always said when she promised she would be fine.

When Mom first got her diagnosis of fibroid tumors, it's funny what things popped into my head. In *Mysteries of the Strange and Unexplained*, I read about Queen Mary of England, who thought she was pregnant twice, but both pregnancies vanished without a trace. She supposedly had giant fibroid tumors instead—tumors in her belly growing big as a basketball. I kept wondering how big Mom's tumors might get before they operated on her.

Once, right after Mom went to the doctors for the first time, I found a wadded-up towel on the bathroom with blood all over it. It made me think of when Malaka threw a vanilla candle at me so I could smell it, but it hit me in the nose instead. Blood gushed out and turned my white shirt red. That's how much blood was on that towel.

I asked Mom about the towel and she said she was fine.

There's more trivia about tumors than you might think. I didn't realize how much until Mom got diagnosed, and then a bunch of it popped into my head like it had been stacked on shelves at the back of my brain until I needed it. There was a man in Vietnam who had a two-hundred-pound tumor removed from his leg—it had been growing for twenty-eight years. I think he turned out to be okay. There was a woman over eight feet tall from Missouri who was already over six feet tall by the time she was my age. Scientists now think it was a tumor on the pituitary gland that caused her to grow that big.

People used to think sharks couldn't get tumors, but it turns out they can.

Goldfish with tumors were once highly prized by Japanese royalty.

Tumors are strange and mysterious things. They appear from out of nowhere. I found it impossible to believe that there was nothing to worry about. That Mom was—*poof!*—totally fine again.

I decided I should sit with her just in case that blood splotch turned out to be serious. I liked to watch her sleep, to watch her chest moving up and down. Taking oxygen in and out.

"You don't need to stay in here," said Mom, her eyes starting to droop. "Go have some fun. Get outside. Go to the park. See some friends. Oh, here's an idea: Do your homework."

"Done," I said. "I'll just sit here another minute."

"'Kay," she said, slurring a little, eyes totally closed. She rolled onto her side, wrapping her arms around herself, like she was giving herself a hug. She always slept like that.

I eased off the bed, not wanting to disturb her, and scooted against the wall. I rested my chin on my knees and watched my mother breathe. Thoughts of Plantagenet High School danced through my head, like sugar plums in that Christmas poem. Being in my mother's room seemed to give me even bigger, crazier fantasies than usual. Maybe I was focusing on the wrong story: The high school might have nothing to do with the writing on the walls.

Plenty of British people had moved to America— there could be descendants of those Plantagenet kings living here in Birmingham. Maybe they were starting a new branch of that snobby club, although it still didn't seem like the kind of club that would promote itself on bathroom walls.

I was more into the idea of the archery society. I hugged my knees closer to myself. Now, really, that could be a clever way to disguise a more interesting kind of club. Archery and horses and medieval weapons. I thought of that article Gram had been reading about the robber who had been hit over the head and left for the police to find. Could there be a group of people out there—secretive, highly trained, of course—fighting crime? I imagined knights in armor clunking criminals over the head with giant hammers.

And what if the alien thing wasn't so crazy? Aliens might consider themselves chosen. Aliens might never grow old. They could have strange powers like that. Powers that meant they'd live forever, that they'd never get sick or hurt or tired.

When Gram came home from work, I was still leaning against the bedroom wall. She apparently called my name a few times before I looked up, because when I finally said "hey," she just shook her head and humphed. I walked back into the living room as she was picking up the purse she'd just set on the coffee table. Then she slipped her feet back into the white sneakers she'd left in the doorway.

"You're coming with me," she said.

Chapter 4

THE FROG GIRL

"We are getting out of this apartment," said Gram. "Now."

She couldn't have surprised me more if she'd announced that she was buying me that pet dolphin I'd always wanted. Gram liked to prop her feet up and flip through the newspaper on the couch after she'd been working for eight hours straight. She never wanted to leave the apartment once she got home. For a few seconds I just stared at her as she opened the front door.

"Come on," she said.

"Where?" I asked.

"You're coming to meet Amelia."

"Who?"

"The girl I told you about. The one who goes to school with you."

"Oh, Gram, that's okay . . ."

She gave me one hard look, purse on her arm, foot tapping. "Grab your coat, Olivia. You've spent way too many afternoons sitting in here alone. It's time to stop thinking so much."

I did not want to go. For more than one reason. First, I did not want to put on my coat. It had belonged to Gram—she hadn't thought the pullover I brought from Charleston was warm enough for early March, and a brand-new coat was another "unnecessary" thing we didn't need to spend money on. The pale green coat was waist-length on Gram, but it was knee-length and baggy on me. It made me look like a lima bean. I usually tried to slip off to school without it, and she usually caught me. I told her I'd rather die of cold than embarrassment, but she did not find it funny.

So I did not want to meet anyone in my lima bean coat. But I also did not want to leave the apartment. I wasn't exactly happy alone in there every afternoon, but I was comfortable. I knew what to expect. I did not want to make awkward conversation with some possibly weird/possibly mean/possibly boring girl. I figured Amelia was probably begging her mother at that very same moment not to force her to make awkward conversation with me. She was probably dreading me coming over. That would make it even worse. I'd have to make conversation with a mean/weird/boring girl who was also annoyed.

But when it all came down to it, nothing I thought really mattered. It was possible that I could have argued with Gram and gotten her to change her mind. I'd say the odds were one in fifty. Arguing with her would have disturbed Mom. And it was always so much work to argue with Gram . . . it was a lot easier just to grab my coat.

"Do you want to push the button?" Gram asked as we stepped into the elevator.

"I'm eleven, Gram," I reminded her, for possibly the thousandth time since we'd moved in. "I don't need to push buttons anymore."

"Suit yourself," she said as the doors closed behind us. "I like pushing them myself."

She was very slow, though, when it came to reaching for the button. Too slow. I admit it—I pushed it. I pushed it twice.

Gram nodded approvingly.

"Your mother is fine, you know," she said as we started to move.

"That's what she always says," I said.

"That's because it's true."

"Okay," I said, a little too quickly. A little too agreeably. Gram frowned like she recognized the tone of someone who doesn't believe you but doesn't want to argue about it. She had Mom's light brown eyes with little gold flecks in them, and when she stared at you, it was hard to look away.

Ding, went the elevator as we passed the third floor. *Ding* again as we passed the second floor.

"I know you were scared when she got sick," she said. "I know you felt like you had to take care of her when it was just the two of you. But you don't have to be scared now. You don't have to worry. She's healing, and, in another month or so, she'll be totally back to normal. You need to stop sitting around imagining that something terrible is going to happen."

"I don't think about terrible things happening," I said.

The elevator was going really slow.

"Of course you don't," she said, a little too quickly.

She didn't say anything else, though; she just stepped out of the elevator when it opened onto the parking level. I followed her and hoped we were done with serious conversations.

It turned out that Amelia lived in a part of town called Southside. We slowed down in front of a white brick house with black shutters and a porch that wrapped around both sides. There was a wrought-iron gate all the way around the house, and the front yard was overgrown and junglelike in a good way, with big shady trees and hanging vines that were already a summery green. The roof had swoops and curves in it, not just straight lines. The front door was polished wood with a big brass knocker in the shape of a fist. It felt weird to pull up to the house in a car—it seemed like the kind of house that would fit better with a horse and carriage. I half expected Amelia and her mother to come out in long puffy dresses and big hats.

Instead they opened the door in jeans and sweatshirts. They were both short—"petite" as Gram would say—with round, happy faces. Mrs. Glasgow was smiling, which looked like her natural expression. Amelia wasn't smiling, but she wasn't frowning either. It looked like she could go either way.

Gram introduced me, and I shook hands with Mrs. Glasgow and then nodded at Amelia.

"Hey," I said, pulling off my coat as quickly as possible.

"Hey," said Amelia, looking at a spot just over my left shoulder. I wasn't sure if she was shy or rude or just uninterested.

Gram rolled her eyes, and Mrs. Glasgow smiled.

"Amelia, why don't you go show Olivia the backyard?" Mrs. Glasgow said, giving Amelia a sort of half-pat, half-shove with one hand.

"Okay, okay," said Amelia, taking a step away from her mother. She met my eyes, finally, and she almost smiled. "Come on. You'll like the backyard. Everyone likes the backyard."

She took off into the house, and I followed. She didn't turn back around until we'd gone through the front door, rounded a corner, walked through the kitchen, passed through a screened-in back porch, and jogged down another set of stairs. Then she stopped and watched me while I took in the backyard.

It was like nothing I had ever seen. It was a big yard with lots of open space, and it was unusually flat for a yard in Birmingham, which is just one hill after another. But what mostly stood out about the view from Amelia's back porch was the boxes. There must have been at least twenty white boxes all over the yard. The best way to describe them is to say they were like white coffins without tops. They were wooden rectangles sticking up out of the ground, no more than a couple of feet tall, but long enough that I could have laid down in them and had a few inches leftover. I couldn't see anything but dirt and grass inside them.

"They're for my frogs," said Amelia, looking very serious.

"Frogs?"

"Yeah. I collect them. As pets."

I walked over to the white box nearest to us. I could see one frog, but there were a couple of tree branches blocking a lot of the ground, so I could have missed others. There was a bowl of water fitted into a hole in the ground, so it looked like a miniature swimming pool.

"I keep leaves and branches for shade and to give them something to hop over, because frogs need their exercise. Plus they all have water," Amelia said from behind me.

It was all so unusual that I forgot to be nervous about talking. My words didn't freeze up.

"Don't they die being trapped in there with no food?" I asked.

"Oh, I feed them spiders and grasshoppers and whatever bugs I find," she said. "Plus they can catch their own food. And they don't drink the water . . ."

"They absorb it into their skin," I finished for her.

She looked at me like I was a potentially interesting frog to add to her collection. "Yeah. How'd you know?"

I shrugged. "I don't know. It's something I remembered. Like how there's one frog that has fake eyes on its butt to confuse predators. And that there's a male frog that swallows frog eggs until they hatch in his throat, then he spits out the babies."

She nodded, impressed. "So you're into frogs?"

"Not especially," I said. "But they're kind of cool. So why do you keep them?"

She looked around, even up at the sky and under the porch, like someone could be eavesdropping from anywhere. The wind blew just as she started to speak, lifting her long dark hair off her neck.

"Because they might be magic," she whispered. "If you catch enough of them, one's bound to be a handsome prince. Or a powerful wizard."

I started planning my escape then. I didn't want to be rude, but I was not going to spend any longer than I had to with a girl with believed frogs could turn into people.

"Yeah, well, uhhh . . ." I looked back toward the house. "I think I hear my grandma calling me. Maybe I should just. . . ."

She laughed out loud. "I'm just messing with you. I want to be a scientist one day, and I really like frogs. I like all amphibians, really, but frogs are the most interesting."

She sat down on the bottom porch step and patted the space next to her. She was still smiling, and she didn't look insane. So I sat next to her and considered what she'd said. I'd never heard of a frog scientist, but it was definitely less crazy than trying to hatch a prince out of one of them.

"So you do experiments on them?" I asked.

"I'm not Dr. Frankenstein," she said. "I don't dissect them or torture them. I keep four frogs in each pen, and I keep a journal of what they eat, how high they hop, which ones seem to get along, and which ones avoid each other. Basically I let them do their own thing, and I just watch them."

"You're not trying to prove anything? Test any theories?"

"Well, I guess you could say I'm collecting data first. I figure before I come up with any major scientific breakthroughs, I need to know what I'm talking about. So I watch."

That seemed very reasonable.

"You kind of freaked me out," I said. "With the whole handsome prince thing."

"That was the point."

"Were you trying to scare me off?"

"My mom told me some lady from work was bringing over her granddaughter. That sounded like it might be boring. Who likes boring?"

I glanced out over all the white rectangles and the thick green grass. You could still see tidy lawnmower tracks in it. A tiny frog head popped up in one box. It disappeared, then popped up again. I saw its glassy, googly eyes and thought maybe it was wondering who I was.

"I thought your frog pens were coffins at first," I admitted.

"Really?" Amelia looked delighted. "Coffins, huh? I can make that work, I think. I have some cousins coming next month. They can be *really* boring if I don't plan ahead."

"Who are you going to say is buried in the coffins?" I asked, curious.

She glanced around the backyard, drumming her fingers against her thigh.

"Well, no one," she said finally. "Because they don't have tops. So that wouldn't work. But maybe, oh . . . maybe whoever was in them has gotten out."

We looked at each other.

"Vampires," we said at the same time.

And that's when I knew we were going to be friends. I had that sensation like I might float off the ground again, like I did walking back from school this afternoon. I tried to shake it off—I didn't want to act like a dork. I didn't want to act like it had been forever since I'd made a new friend. But it was a nice feeling.

That's all I'm saying. It was nice.

Amelia reached under the porch stairs and pulled out a thick, hardbound notebook so stuffed with papers that it looked like the binding might burst. She showed me how she had photos of each frog, neatly labeled with its name. She'd made notes every day on every frog's behavior, line after line of her squished-up handwriting saying things like, "10:30 a.m.: Eugene ate entire cricket. 4 p.m.: Has not moved from same spot in corner of box for at least four hours." And, "9 a.m.: Delores attempted to escape. Threw herself at the wall repeatedly. 1:15 p.m.: Delores made it halfway over the wall. Got stuck. Do not know how long she was hanging there until I found her. Seems stunned but okay."

"Eugene? Delores?" I asked.

"I try to pick good frog names," she said. She flipped through the pages until she came to a snapshot that had been pasted in the middle of a page. "Sometimes I take extra pictures, you know, if any of them do something especially memorable."

The page read, "Alexander, May 6." The picture showed a frog lying on its back, legs straight up in the air.

"Is he dead?" I asked.

"No. He's just relaxing. He flipped back over a few minutes later. Maybe it was some sort of stretching exercise. Or maybe he had a bad back. I dunno. But

I keep the camera here just in case they do anything spectacular," she said.

I read through her notebook, more and more impressed. As I read, I could occasionally hear a frog thump against a wooden wall. The porch steps creaked anytime we shifted, and the sound made me think of rocking chairs.

"You know what I said about frogs being magic?" said Amelia, playing with the buttons on her camera. "I know they're not, but it'd be cool, wouldn't it? If all you had to do to get your heart's desire was to kiss a frog. It'd be gross, but it'd be worth it, wouldn't it?"

I closed the notebook and handed it back. "I don't think you get a wish when you kiss the frog. I think it just turns into a prince. I think you're confusing it with rubbing a genie's bottle."

Amelia shook her finger at me. "Oh, there are lots of magic frog stories. They're not always princes. Sometimes it's a girl who's the frog. Sometimes it's a magician in disguise. A frog could be anybody."

I didn't feel like I had enough expertise with frog stories to argue with her. And it was kind of a pleasant idea. Tons of important people disguising themselves as frogs. I had a vision of walking over to one of Amelia's frog boxes, picking up a frog, and having it suddenly turn into a man in a suit, holding a briefcase and a business card. "I'm Thaddeus Whitehead, and I've handled hundreds of lawsuits," he'd say, like one of those lawyers on television commercials. "Right now I'm a frog. But while you're here, have you ever been in car accident? Were you injured on the job? Would you like to sue anyone? Ribbit?"

Amelia cracked her knuckles next to me.

"So what would you wish for?" she asked. "If you got one wish?"

I looked away from the box where Thaddeus Whitehead, frog-lawyer, might be rolling in the mud.

"Right now?" I asked. "A huge cup of coffee."

She looked disappointed. "You're not taking it seriously."

I made the sound of a daddy frog horking up a few dozen tadpoles. "*You* are getting on *me* for making a joke?"

"You should take wishes seriously," she said. "I always have mine planned out. Just in case."

"So what's your one wish?" I asked.

I don't know what I expected her to say. To be able to fly? To read minds? I was pretty sure she was a girl who liked the idea of superpowers. But she surprised me.

"I'd like to build a colony on the moon," she said. "With rocket ships that took off from airports all across the world, so all sorts of people could go up and visit. Not just astronauts or rich people. Everyone. And it'd be spectacular up there—flying cars and giant swimming pools in the moon craters. Big silver skyscrapers that float."

"And anyone could go?" I asked. "Like for a weekend?"

"Yeah, that's the point. Even if you're stuck here on plain Earth, you should be able to see it. Even if you're, like, a teacher who talks about spelling all day long, you should be able to put your head down on your desk and remember swimming pools on the moon. You'd have that little bit of spectacular with you wherever you went. Oh, look, Brunhilda is trying to catch that fly!"

I watched her sprint over to Brunhilda with her camera, thinking how she focused so calmly and completely on those frogs. Like she wouldn't stop until she knew the answers. I thought that maybe, even if she never got a magic wish, she would be the one who figured out how to build a moon colony. She seemed like she could solve any puzzle.

"Hey, Amelia," I said, once the fly had escaped from Brunhilda and flown off to a frog-free part of the yard. "I want to tell you something."

So I told her all of it. That first time I saw "Plantagenet" written on the wall at Trattoria Centrale. The message in the bathroom at school. The results of my Google search. She didn't say much. She just nodded and listened, which is probably exactly what a good scientist would do.

"So what would you do?" I asked. "If you wanted to know what it meant?"

"You need more data," she announced. "That's the problem. You're trying to put together a hypothesis when you don't even know all the facts."

"I don't know where to look."

"Yes, you do. But you need to look more. You need to branch out. Be organized about it."

"What do you mean?" I asked.

"I'll show you," she said, and she held up her camera.

Chapter 5

THE DATA

The next day after school, I skipped Trattoria Centrale and instead took a roundabout way to Gram's that wound along 1st and 2nd Avenues. I stopped in every restaurant or shop that I thought might have a public restroom. A couple of cashiers shook their heads at me when I asked to go to the bathroom, but most people smiled and waved me toward the back of the store.

Not that it was easy. Walking up to complete strangers and asking anything—even just for the bathroom—didn't come very naturally to me in my new Birmingham life. But I felt a little less shy and a little more comfortable knowing that all along 3rd and 4th Avenues, Amelia was doing the same thing.

I had a partner now.

Even after just a month in town, I had a good sense

of all the coffee shops and bakeries near me—Urban Standard, Celestial Realm, La Reunion, Lucy's, Crestwood Coffee. But I'd pretty much only paid attention to places where I could buy sweets and drinks. That afternoon I got a crash course in just how many stores and bathrooms there were within ten city blocks.

Less than an hour after school got out, I'd been in six restaurants, three ladies boutiques, two antique stores, two drugstores, one ice-cream place, a jewelry store, and a corner grocery store. I'd looked over the bathrooms from ceilings to floors (some of which, let me just say, were cleaner than others). I'd read some things I wish I hadn't, but I'd also found what Amelia and I had hoped I'd find—more mentions of Plantagenet.

She'd been right—I'd needed to branch out more. I'd needed to gather more data. My heels had blisters on them, and my back was wet with cold sweat, but as I trudged the last couple of blocks to Gram's, I was stuffed full of data. And since I'd also followed Amelia's advice and taken photos of the walls, I had permanent records of everything I'd seen, easy to pull out and study in bed or at school or wherever. I could hardly wait to print everything out, and Gram's camera—old, but still digital, at least—felt like it was nudging my hip with every step I took.

Every few steps I wedged that camera a little farther down in my pocket. I guarded it like secret treasure.

It's not that I had so many photos. I'd probably taken fewer than a dozen, since I didn't find the words in every bathroom. But I'd found a version of the two sentences I'd first seen in Trattoria in five more stalls.

I didn't think of them as sentences anymore, though.

I thought of them as messages.

I was so excited that I couldn't believe I was walking along the sidewalk like it was any other afternoon—I felt like I should float right up to the rooftops. My hands were tingly. My lips kept wanting to pull into a smile.

All the sounds on the street were sharper than usual, like I had become super aware of everything. A car honked, and a bell jingled as someone opened a door. A pigeon cooed somewhere above me, and a UPS truck rumbled by, clunking over a pothole. I'd walked these streets dozens of times, and they'd always seemed dull and empty. Now they were packed with excitement and possibility. Every person I passed could be my mystery writer. Every little sight or sound could be a clue.

I tried to settle down, partly because I wanted to think about what I'd found, and partly because I'd already accidentally run into a nice little old lady because I was trying to read some writing on the side of a building. (For the record, it was pigeon poop, not writing.) I'd added some important pieces of the puzzle in the last hour. The messages were all in the same handwriting, and they were all written in purple.

I'd also realized that someone was making a habit of writing in the *women's* bathrooms. (Not that I could check the men's rooms.) I'd found the sentence in two ladies' clothing stores and one jewelry store. Plus, the writing looked feminine. It all pointed to a girl or a woman.

If she wasn't just some girl at my school—and I really didn't think she was, or, at least, I really didn't want her to be—she probably either lived or worked around here, because why else would she be leaving messages in this neighborhood? Or maybe she was driving all over the city and had left messages in hundreds of bathrooms. I couldn't rule that out. But I knew the writer had to have been around here often, going in and out of stores and restaurants. Maybe she was still here, still passing me on the street while I walked home from school.

The biggest question, of course, more interesting than *who* was writing the messages, was *why*.

What did it all mean?

That, by the way, is exactly what Amelia asked me the next day. I watched for her in the halls on my way to homeroom, and it was the first time since Charleston that I'd had someone to look for in the halls. A little past the school office, I spotted her and called her name. She jogged over to me, weaving through all the other kids. She didn't bother with a hello.

"There was that exact same Plantagenet message in a sewing store and a Mexican restaurant!" she said. "I'll show you on my camera."

"I found five more," I said. "I don't think we have time to look at pictures before the bell rings, though."

She bounced impatiently.

"It's aliens," she said, her book bag slapping against her back. "I know it."

"You just want help with your moon colony."

"Maybe. Doesn't mean it's not aliens."

"I'll call you," I said. "Maybe we can get together tomorrow? I don't want to be late to homeroom."

"We're talking about an alien invasion and the future of the world," she said, turning toward her own class, "and you're worried about being *late*?"

"Invasion?" I said.

"Don't you watch any movies?" she called over her shoulder.

I wasn't late at all. I had still had five minutes before the bell. But, for the first time, I had no problem filling the time before class started.

I didn't need to fidget with pages and pretend to be busy. I had plenty to do without pretending. I held the camera in both hands. I scanned through my photos, enlarging them on the screen, moving them around. I was going to be as thorough and patient as Amelia with her frogs—I would study every picture. I would memorize every detail. The camera let me spread out all my evidence and take my time, calm and collected, no emotion at all.

Well, that had been the idea at least. Honestly, I was having a hard time keeping calm. And forget about no emotion. Because the photos had already shown me a couple of things that I missed the first time around. I guess I'd been so excited at first that I hadn't really looked closely. And the lighting in most bathrooms wasn't the best.

But now something was obvious: The Plantagenet messages weren't all the same.

With Rachel and her friends chatting behind me— about shoes, and mothers, and apparently a really gross dead roach—I flipped through my photos in order of how I'd found the messages. First, I looked at the picture I'd taken from one wall at Trattoria.

Nothing had changed there—it was the original message. *We are Plantagenet. We are chosen.*

Next I studied the picture of the school bathroom

wall, which had the same message as Trattoria, but with the additional line.

We are Plantagenet. We are chosen.

We will never grow old.

Now this was where it started getting interesting. When I looked at the photo from Levy's jewelry store, I saw something below the "We are Plantagenet" line I'd first seen. There was a water stain on the wall and some scribbling by a black pen, but underneath it all, there was more faded purple writing.

We are Plantagenet.

We walk next to you.

But we are not one of you.

There was something even more interesting from the Urban Standard coffeehouse. It was so small I hadn't seen it at first. It wasn't in the usual purple pen. It was written in a plain blue ink, and it was easy to miss on the beige walls. But this was the message that made my heart beat a little faster.

We are Plantagenet.

Our home is in the stars.

I thought back to that ridiculous website about aliens, with its talk of a crashed ship and helpful blue-eyed, silver-haired aliens. No matter how much Amelia loved the idea, I knew aliens were ridiculous. But still . . . maybe. On a wall inside my brain, that

was the word I kept writing over and over: "Maybe."

I wouldn't take it further than that. But I kept rereading the lines I'd found, considering what a home in the stars might mean. People (or something like people) who never grew old, who were not really like us. Who were smarter, stronger, better. Who never got sick, never got hurt, never got tired. . . .

Maybe.

I felt a hand land on my shoulder, and the pressure startled me enough that I dropped the camera on the floor. Luckily, it seemed pretty sturdy. I bent to pick it up, turning in my desk to look into Rachel's slightly surprised face.

"Sorry," she said. "I didn't mean to make you jump."

She had blue eyes, it occurred to me. Not that I was looking. Not that I was suddenly very interested in blue eyes.

"I wasn't paying attention," I said, inconspicuously looking for any silver streaks in her brown hair. "My fault."

As I spoke, I realized I hadn't frozen up at all. In fact, my words seemed to be coming easier all the time. My head was full of thoughts of Plantagenet and Amelia. I hadn't even remembered to be embarrassed about my lima bean coat that morning.

"I was just going to ask you about your pictures," Rachel said. "What are they?"

Well, there was no way to answer that and not have it sound weird. I considered my options. . . .

"Glad you asked, Rachel. These are messages from aliens."

"Well, Rachel, there's this secret society of people who use medieval weapons, and they could be using bathrooms as their home base."

"I think some kings of England are spending a lot of time in the toilet."

I finally just shrugged—inside my head, not in real life. I had nothing to lose. It wasn't like she wanted to be friends with me anyway. She had plenty of friends; she didn't need more. I picked the best of all my creepy possible response.

"They're pictures of bathroom walls," I said.

"Huh," she said. "Why do you like bathroom walls?"

I turned all the way around in my seat. No one had ever asked me that. I hadn't ever had an actual conversation about the appeal of bathroom walls. I was surprised to realize that I knew the answer: It was waiting there on my tongue.

"Because what people write can be really interesting," I said. "It's like they pull random thoughts out of their head and leave them on the wall, and then, when you come along, you get to read their thoughts. You get to look inside people's heads for just a second."

"Like a crystal ball," she said.

"Sort of," I said.

"You ever played with a Ouija board?" she asked. "My mom won't let me have one, but I tried it last summer at somebody else's house. I asked it the name of who I would marry."

"Did it tell you?" I asked, interested.

"Yes," she whispered, leaning closer.

"Who?"

"Blarktog."

I started to giggle, and she did, too.

"Blarktog?" I asked.

"It actually spelled B-L-R-K-T-G, so I added some vowels." She tried to keep a straight face. "I think he might be Russian."

Mrs. Snellhawk started talking then, so I had to face forward. I was pretty sure that was the most sentences I'd ever exchanged with anybody at my new school. And it hadn't been awkward. I'd felt normal. Like my old self. That was the kind of conversation I might have had in Charleston. (Evon and I had once played with a Ouija board. Evon asked it where she would live when she grew up. It answered, "A big mushroom." I admit—there was nothing magic about it. I was totally steering the game piece. The best part was when we got to "A big m . . ." and she was sure it was going to say mansion.)

After school, I went for my usual water and scone. I couldn't see Amelia until after school the next day— she had gymnastics on Thursdays—and I wanted to visit Trattoria's bathroom again, the place where everything started. Like I'd told Rachel, I loved feeling as if there were countless strangers talking to me, telling me bits and pieces about their lives, expecting me to make sense of them.

I slipped into the bathroom, just standing there, sipping my coffee, considering the walls. Trying to imagine who wrote the words, imagining what she meant, what she wanted. Did she think about who would read them? Did she mean them as a message at all?

"Who are you, Plantagenet?" I whispered at the wall.

As many words as the wall had on it, it didn't have any answers for me.

I had my book bag with me, and there was a pen in it. I thought of the other verses I'd seen around town. And I had a really intense need to see them all together. To see the whole thing written out smooth and whole, like a poem. I found the darkest pen I had, and I wrote

in block letters underneath the original "We are Plantagenet. We are chosen." By the time I finished, I had a
significant block of the wall covered. It read:

We are Plantagenet. We are chosen.

WE WILL NEVER GROW OLD.

WE ARE PLANTAGENET.

WE WALK NEXT TO YOU.

BUT WE ARE NOT ONE OF YOU.

WE ARE PLANTAGENET.

OUR HOME IS IN THE STARS.

When I got back to my seat, I noticed I had
ink on my hands, and I didn't want to clean it
off. There was something nice about leaving a
message. I'd never left one myself before. It felt
satisfying. Important. I had my own words there—
well, sort of my own words—jammed in with a
million other words. I hadn't just left a message—I
was part of something. I'd added my mark to all the
other marks, and even though I didn't know the people
who'd written on the wall, my words were part of theirs
now. I was permanent. I was unerasable.

AUSTRALIA RULES

FeeL DON'T ThinK

Ella & Jenn

Team Kennedy (NEW ORLEANS) loves Zaza

Your future is Bright!

WAR EAGLE

HANG ROCK

We are Plantagenet. We are chosen.
WE WILL NEVER GROW OLD.
WE ARE PLANTAGENET.
WE WALK NEXT TO YOU.
BUT WE ARE NOT ONE OF YOU.
WE ARE PLANTAGENET.
OUR HOME IS IN THE STARS.

It's 8:45 on a Sun

VIVA MEXICO!

PEOP

Chapter 6

COUCH REST

When I got home, I was surprised to find Mom on the couch. She gave a cheerful little wave when I walked through the door.

"The days of taking it easy are over," she said as I leaned down to hug her. "Checked off the list. Now I'm supposed to get some real exercise."

"Exercise?" I didn't think she looked like she was in any shape for swimming.

"Well, move around more, at least," she said. "I'm supposed to stretch my muscles a little. Walk up and down the stairs if I can."

"Is that safe? Shouldn't you maybe just walk around the couch a little?"

"No, Dr. Mario, I do not need to do laps around the couch. According to my actual doctor, exercise is

66

totally safe. And necessary. If I don't work my muscles, I won't heal as well."

Well, that changed things. I wanted her to heal perfectly. Quickly. Permanently. And if she needed exercise, I could help.

"You want to try a flight of stairs?" I asked. "I'll hold your arm."

So that's how we wound up in the stairwell, surrounded by concrete walls and concrete floor and concrete ceiling, both of us blowing wispy puffs in the cold air every time we exhaled because the stairwells weren't heated. Mom was doing pretty well—she'd done fine going down one flight, and she was working her way back up to our floor now. Her bare feet were completely silent on the stairs. Her arm was looped around my shoulders, and I had an arm around her waist. I thought she felt too light. Wispy as a puff of air.

"Hey, I could go get you a milk shake when we get back upstairs," I said. I was barefoot, too—neither one of us ever liked shoes—and my toes were starting to get numb from the icy concrete. "Or hot chocolate. Or there's that cupcake place down the street."

"Gram will definitely think those are unnecessary expenses," she said, pausing between the words, catching her breath. She was leaning a little more heavily on me with each step. I counted five more stairs left.

"Are you . . ." she started to ask. Three more steps. "Are you trying to fatten me up?"

"Maybe," I said. "I think you've lost some weight."

One stair left. No stairs left. Her arm lifted off my shoulder, and I straightened once the weight was gone. I didn't realize I'd been stooping. I lifted my arms over my head and stretched, enjoying the pull all the way from my back to my fingertips.

Mom stood with the stairwell door open, doing her own more subtle stretches. Tilting her head from side to side, flexing and pointing her toes. She watched me and frowned.

"I put too much weight on you, didn't I? You're sore?"

"I'm fine," I said.

She raised an eyebrow, head still cocked to the side from rolling her neck. "I thought that was my line," she said.

We padded back down the hallway, both of us glad to be off the cold concrete and onto the soft carpet. After Mom unlocked the door, she took both my hands in hers and pulled me to the sofa.

"We need to talk, Mario," she said.

I couldn't help it—I jerked my hands away from her and scooted back, scooted as far away from her as I could get. My skin felt tight all of a sudden, and I felt a small earthquake run through me, a shiver from my lips to my fingers.

Those were the exact words she'd used after she hung up with the doctor's office in Charleston. *We need to talk.*

Mom winced and ran a hand over her face. I could see she remembered, too.

"Sorry, sweetheart," she said. "Bad choice of words. It's nothing bad. Don't worry."

Why was everyone always telling me that? As if two words were all it took to change the thoughts running through your mind. As if you could just tell yourself, "Stop worrying, self," and all the bad thoughts would evaporate and instead your head would be filled with rainbows and flowers and unicorns.

"I want to apologize," Mom said, and that got my attention. It made no sense. She had nothing to apologize for.

"I leaned on you too much in Charleston," she said, settling herself deeper into the couch. "I was scared and I felt bad, and I let you take care of me more than you should have. And that's not the way it should be. I'm the mother; you're the daughter. I take care of you. Not the other way around."

I stared at her. At her tired eyes and bird-nest hair and face that was sweaty from walking up one flight of stairs. And she was telling me I shouldn't take care of her? That I shouldn't protect her?

Of course I should. Someone had to protect her. Someone had to keep her safe. And if she was telling me that I shouldn't do it, it must mean that I'd done a very bad job of it. I hadn't made her feel safe. Even though I'd tried to be strong and happy and keep my face smooth and smiling, I must have let the cracks show. She must have noticed that sometimes I didn't feel strong and happy. And now she was worried about me. On top of herself.

I'd screwed it all up.

She just kept talking.

"I'm getting better now," she said, "and things are going to go back to the way they were before I got sick. You don't need to stay home with me. You don't need to go get me ice cream or medicine or offer to rub my feet or fix my hair. You are no longer on nurse duty. You are on eleven-year-old-girl duty."

Those last few weeks in Charleston, this is how I started the morning: I woke up at six a.m., without an alarm clock, and I woke up fast. I've always had an alarm clock in my head. One minute I was dead asleep, and then my eyes flew open and I sat up in bed. Not groggy, not blurry-eyed. Totally awake. You know how a dog can be snoring on the floor one second, and then—maybe you open the door or something—it jumps up and wags its tail so fast you think it was faking sleep in the first place? That's how I was. And the second my feet hit the ground, I headed to Mom's room. She usually slept a little later, but I would creep over to her bed and be sure her chest was moving. If I couldn't tell, I would put my hand under her nose to feel the little snorts of air. Then, once I knew she was alive, I would go make her toast. Two pieces, no butter. And tea, not coffee, because coffee made her stomach get upset.

And every morning, when I brought the tray into her room, she would tell me not to do it anymore, that I didn't need to make her breakfast. That she could get it herself. But she'd eat every bite of the toast. And drink every sip of the tea. And it felt so good to know that I was helping, that I was doing something. That maybe, if she had a full belly from toast and tea, it would make her stronger. It would make her better.

If I hadn't been able to make her toast every morning, I think I would have screamed. Or broken things. Or run out the door and kept running until my legs gave out. Because I had to do something while she was lying in bed so still.

Mom was still talking.

"And especially after your father," she said. "You'd already had to . . ."

I jumped off the sofa then. Actually jumped off of it. I ran to the front door, then remembered I didn't have anywhere to go. Trattoria would close any minute. Gram would be home soon, expecting me to be there. There wasn't even a door on my bedroom. But I just wanted to leave. I wanted to be by myself, without walls around me and doors closing me in. Sometimes I thought the condo was too small to hold enough air for all three of us. I'd wake up in the middle of the night gasping, sweating. Sometimes in the middle of the day, with sunlight pouring in from the windows, I still felt like gasping, like I'd been underwater for too long and I was kicking and kicking as fast as I could and I'd die if I didn't break the surface of the water soon.

This was one of those gasping moments. I had to get out. Before Mom kept talking and talking.

"I'm going to, um, get something I dropped. In the hall. Or somewhere. I won't leave the building," I said as I swung open the door.

"Mario!" yelled Mom. "Wait!"

Then the door swung closed and cut off anything else she might have said. She knew I was lying. I was a terrible liar at the best of moments, and that whole

I dropped something was not my cleverest moment. But I knew I was safe. I felt guilty as I ran down the hallway, but I knew she couldn't come after me. She could barely walk, much less run.

I wound up back in the stairwell, which was every bit as cold as the outdoors, trudging up and up and up. My thighs burned. This time the winter air felt crisp and good as it bit into my skin. I liked how it stung my throat and the inside of my nose. It was like taking a cold shower without needing water. When I ran out of stairs, I tucked myself into a ball on the top floor of the building, my knees against my chest, my back pressing against the concrete.

I had a place of my own in Charleston. A few blocks from our apartment was a church built in the 1800s. If you were walking down the sidewalk, you'd pass the church, then an ice-cream shop, then a lawyer's office. And if you didn't know it was there, you might completely miss an iron gate on the side of the church that led to what looked like an overgrown garden.

It wasn't a garden, though—it was an old cemetery. Once you got through the iron gate, a stone path twisted through trees and vines, palmettos and monkey grass. In some spots, sunshine hit the ground like a spotlight. But mostly the trees kept all the tombstones shaded. The magnolia trees were the biggest I've ever seen, and in spring, the blooms filled up the air with the smell of lemon and honey.

The gravestones were the real reason I loved to go there. They stood up like dominoes all through the grass and weeds. I'd first visited the cemetery on a field trip at my old school; the teachers taught us how to do gravestone rubbings. I'd kept my stack of thin papers, the pencil marks gray like stone, even though I'd also etched plenty of the grave markers into my memory. Some had nothing but all-capital last names carved into the stone. JENNINGS. TWOMEY. ST. CROIX. Those were the most mysterious graves— you couldn't tell when the people had lived, how old they'd been when they'd died, or even if they'd been men or women. Lots of the stones at least gave you full names and dates:

LYDA WENTWORTH

June 1, 1834

September 16, 1891

HENRY ADAM ELLS

February 1803

May 1824

But the best stones read like very short stories of people's lives . . .

ALLISTER SOLOMON HANOVER

Born in Charleston

on the thirteenth day of January 1894.

Called by God to minister to the masses in Indonesia.

Lived among his people for forty years, survived

fire and pestilence. Returned to Charleston

after he was called home to God on

the twentieth day of July 1951.

LELA ALVINIA MONROE

February 1822–May 1846

Our darling lived briefly but well, leaving behind

doting parents, a heartbroken husband,

and three daughters who will feel her absence.

She will be missed most by another one

whose name is unwritten.

I spent a lot of time thinking about Allister and Lela. What fire and pestilence did Allister survive? What exactly was pestilence? Was he scarred, wounded? Did he save lives? Did he ask to be brought back to Charleston after he died, or would he rather have stayed in Indonesia? And Lela—what killed her when she was only twenty-four? And—this is the part I wondered most about—who was the one who missed her most, whose name couldn't be written on her gravestone?

And if they wouldn't write the name, why mention the person at all?

In some ways I guess the bathroom stalls reminded me of my cemetery back home. Because even after they've left, people leave bits of themselves behind, pieces of their story. As long as they've left words, they're never really gone. Lela died over 150 years ago, and I still knew her. Thought about her. Even if everybody else forgot, I would remember.

I'd never even seen my dad's gravestone.

Sometimes it'd be nice not to have a memory. To wake up in the morning with your mind scrubbed clean as a Dry Erase Board, white and empty.

As I was sitting there in the empty stairwell, thinking of gravestones and Dry Erase Boards, my butt getting colder and colder through my jeans, I let myself think about *What if.* The big *What if* that I had been trying to keep myself from considering. What if the possibilities I'd told myself were crazy were actually true? What if the Plantagenets were magical—if they were aliens or a secret club or whatever—and they had some kind of special powers?

Maybe the Plantagenets wrote on the walls because they wanted to be found. And if you found them, they could do all sorts of wonderful things. Make all your wishes come true. Make anything happen. Or unhappen.

Maybe.

As Amelia would say, I needed more data. The only question was where to find it. And I was beginning to think I had a decent guess.

Gram was waiting for me on the sofa when I finally let myself back into the condo. I didn't see Mom.

"Good day?" Gram asked, sipping a glass of water.

"Sure," I said.

"That's why you were out there lurking on the stairs?"

"I wasn't lurking."

"Your mom says you disappeared nearly an hour ago."

She patted the sofa next to her, and I didn't see any easy way to avoid sitting down for more talking. But when I eased onto the cushions, folding my legs up under me, Gram didn't say anything. She turned back to the television, which had some dumb judge show on it. I hate judge shows. The judges are always so sure of themselves. Just once I'd like to hear one of them say, *"Hmm, that's a tough one. I don't know. I tell you what—I'm thinking of a number between one and a hundred. Whoever guesses closest wins. Loser goes to jail. Case dismissed."*

That's how things are really decided, isn't it? Just luck or no luck.

"Homework?" asked Gram after a while.

"Finished," I said. "And no tests tomorrow."

"You see Amelia at school today?"

"Uh-huh."

"I did good, didn't I? I told you you'd like her."

We'd sort of already been through this—I'd told Gram when we drove back from Amelia's that we'd had fun. I'd said I liked her. I'd said we were going to hang out again. But Gram wasn't letting it go. She liked to hear how right she'd been.

"I know," I said, trying to smile. "I'm glad you introduced me to her."

"You still hoping to go over to her place tomorrow?"

I didn't want to get into that quite yet. "I think so. Or we might go somewhere else, I guess. I'm going to call her tonight."

The judge on television banged her gavel, and Gram was quiet for a while.

"You should go talk to your mom," she said.

I just kept looking at the television.

"She asked me to send you into her room."

Gram flexed her bare feet back and forth like they were bothering her. Her ankles looked swollen.

"And she said to tell you that you didn't have to

talk," she added. "Or that you could talk about how many times the average human blinks in a day. Something like that. I never know what you two mean."

"Okay," I said, relieved. "I know what she means."

No more Dad conversation. I felt my mood improve a little bit.

Gram nodded, either at me or at the television.

"You know," she said, "these poor people come on this show and let that judge ask them all sorts of questions and insult them and order them around. Don't you wonder why anyone would ever come on this program?"

"Yes," I said, because I had always wondered that exact thing.

"I think," she said, "that it's because people just need to talk. They get stuff built up inside them, and they need to let it out. They need somebody to listen. Even if they don't know it."

"I don't think that's it," I said.

I stood up and turned away from the television.

Chapter 7

WHAT THE TREE TOLD US

It was easier than I thought it would be to get a ride to the old Plantagenet High School. It turned out that Amelia's mother was used to her daughter requesting rides to strange nooks of the city to look for new frogs. ("Once she took me to the Cahaba River three times in one week," Amelia told me over the phone. "She'll just be happy I want to go someplace where the car won't get stuck in the mud and have to be towed.")

When we pulled up in front of what used to be the high school, I thought we might have a problem. My mom had been right when she said there was almost nothing left of the school. Plantagenet High was on an abandoned lot, with a concrete path leading from the sidewalk to what probably used to be the front entrance. Now it was a path to a big blank space. I could barely make out the edges of the concrete foundation because of the tall weeds.

A little ways away from the foundation, there was a broken sign with the name of the school, but some of the letters had fallen off. The unmowed weeds and grass covered everything. And buried in the grass, like really disappointing Easter eggs, were years' worth of aluminum cans and paper cups, bits of cardboard and decomposing paper. The whole scene was dirty and ugly and more than a little depressing.

"Are you girls sure you want to poke around here?" asked Amelia's mom, slowing to a stop.

"Yes, ma'am," I said.

"It seems a little iffy," she said, frowning. "But I'll park here and keep an eye on you. Try not to stay too long. Don't get out of view of the car."

"It's just a scouting mission," said Amelia. "I'd love to find an Eastern spadefoot."

"I hope when you win the Nobel Prize in frogs, you'll remember to thank me in your acceptance speech," said her mom, shooing us out of the car.

"The spadefoot is a toad, not a frog," said Amelia as she slid across the seat.

I shut the door behind me.

"Nice thinking with that whole spadefoot thing," I said to Amelia.

"What?" she said, scanning the grass at her feet. "I would love an Eastern spadefoot. But I don't think this ground is swampy enough."

As we stood there, just a few inches off the sidewalk, all the confidence and excitement I'd felt in the car seemed to evaporate, drifting away on the wind like dandelion seeds. All I'd thought about for the last twenty-four hours was getting here. It had felt comforting to focus on the high school. Simple. A high school is a nice solid thing. You can touch it. It's not like dreams or plans or mysteries or hopes or secret messages—those are all things that pop like bubbles. Flimsy and full of air.

I'd been clinging to the idea of a good solid clue. I'd hoped—pretended?—that once we got here, my next step would be clear. I guessed I'd hoped that there'd be some giant *X* on the ground or some flashing neon arrow to my next piece of the puzzle. But all I saw was litter and weeds and concrete.

"So we're thinking what?" asked Amelia, kicking an empty Sprite can. "Maybe somebody's spelled out *Plantagenet* with aluminum cans? Maybe there's a secret group of magicians living underground?

Litterbug magicians? Because I don't see anything."

I agreed with her, but I didn't want to give up and go home without taking a single step. Surely we should at least take a quick look around. I considered the view once more. The cement walkway winding its way to nothing. The sad blank space where the school used to be. The only pretty thing left was the trees. I think they were oaks. The trunks were wide and rough, and the branches spread out across the lot, reaching toward each other. The leaves of each tree brushed against leaves from the trees around it, and it made me think of holding hands. Like the trees were still sad about what happened to the school, and they were reaching out to comfort one another.

"Let's at least look at the foundation," I said. "Maybe there's more over there than we think. A basement or something. An old storeroom."

"You're a very glass-half-full sort of person," Amelia said.

We waved at Amelia's mom to reassure her, then we walked side by side along the path. Amelia was looking down—probably still holding out hope for an Eastern spadefoot—while I looked around. She was lucky—at least she knew what she was looking for. I kept an eye on the grass, on the concrete, and on the tall rectangular sign off to our left; I even kept an eye on the litter. Because any of it might matter. Any of it might look like a path to nothing and turn out to be a path to something.

We stepped onto the foundation of the school, and once we were in the middle of it, it was just a big gray square. It could have been a basketball court or a playground or a parking lot. I thought there might be burn marks from the fire, but the cement was smooth and unmarked. No signs of old doorways or rooms or stairways or plumbing. Other than litter and leaves, the only thing I saw was a plastic O that must have fallen off the school sign.

I sighed.

"Let's look at the sign," I said. As far as I could tell it was the only thing left that even had the word "Plantagenet" on it.

Well, it almost had the whole word. As we waded through the weeds, I kept an eye out for more fallen letters, which had to be somewhere. The sign actually said:

WELC E TO PLA T NET H GH SCHO L
HOME OF TH GO HERS

"Go hers?" said Amelia. "Oh. Gophers, I guess. Home of the Gophers. That's not a very good mascot. Who's afraid of a gopher?"

I was looking at the base of the sign. I'd really only noticed the plastic board and plastic letters at first, but the bottom of the sign was much more stable and impressive. It was solid stone, and it looked very old. And, as I leaned in closer, I could see words carved into the stone. The letters were faded a little, and the stone was turning black, so I had to strain to read.

"Amelia!" I said. I didn't trust my own eyes. "What does that look like to you?"

She squinted. "Um, it looks like . . . Oh. I think it says, *'We are Plantagenet.'*"

"That's what I thought," I said.

The same words written in purple pen on bathroom walls in the twenty-first century had been carved in this stone ages ago. Maybe back when the high school was built. There was no talk of living forever or living in the stars. But words carved in stone seemed awfully permanent. Awfully sure of themselves. More important, somehow, than words on bathroom walls.

"What do you think?" said Amelia, brushing the stone with her finger. "A high school for aliens?"

"Can we sit down a minute?" I looked around my feet. I was standing by what looked like an old moldy T-shirt. "Or maybe not sit. Maybe walk?"

"Sure," said Amelia. "I wouldn't mind covering more ground anyway."

She kept her head down as we walked, and I thought she was back to thinking of frogs. I felt like I was trying to lace up a new pair of tennis shoes with more laces than I had holes. I'd found something here, all right, but I didn't know how to make it fit.

"Maybe a school motto," said Amelia, who had apparently not been thinking about amphibians. "It was written on that sign like a motto. Like our school's motto is 'Walk don't run.'"

I stopped. "That's our school's motto?"

She shrugged apologetically. "I guess mottoes aren't really the city's strong point."

"Anyway," I said. "That would make sense. A motto. So what are the chances it's a coincidence that the school motto—or whatever it is—just happens to be part of the writing I've seen on the bathroom walls?"

"It's only three words," said Amelia. "Pretty common words, except for the Plantagenet part. But it's still hard to believe it's a coincidence."

I nodded. Hearing her say what I was thinking made the whole situation seem more manageable. More understandable. I'd gotten so used to having conversations by myself, inside my head, that I'd forgotten how helpful it could be to go over a problem with someone.

"I think so, too," I said. "I think someone connected with this school has been writing on the walls."

We were on the edge of the lot now, in the middle of a group of oak trees. The ground was bare, totally shaded by the branches so that grass obviously couldn't grow underneath. The air was cold and crisp, and even in the middle of a city block, somehow it felt quiet and peaceful in the shade. I could hear traffic noise in the background, but I could also hear the rustling of the leaves in the wind.

"Speaking of writing . . . ," said Amelia. She pointed at the tree closest to her. I could make out a smattering of names and initials carved in the wood. There were hearts with arrows through them. The tree was tattooed all over like an NBA player's arm.

"I guess this is what people did before they wrote on walls," I said.

"And when it wasn't illegal to have a knife at school," Amelia added.

I walked to another tree, and there were plenty of carvings in it, too. It was hard to make most of them out—the knife marks were slowly being absorbed back into the wood. The letters looked like they'd been etched a long time ago, and they were fading just like ink did.

I kept exploring until I got to the fifth or sixth tree,

one so big that if Amelia and I stood on either side of it, we couldn't have gotten our arms around it. I squinted to try to make out any letters. I could make out one here or there, and occasionally a word, but then I got to one section where the initials looked fresh. They were at least half an inch deep, as if they'd been carved yesterday.

And the initials were inside a slightly crooked star.

"I don't know," said Amelia, when I'd called her over. "A star? It's not too hard to find a drawing of a star."

"You think it's a coincidence?" I asked. "'*Our home is in the stars?*'"

"Yes, I do think it's a coincidence. Otherwise, oh, the American flag might also be a clue. Or those little glow-in-the-dark designs you stick on your ceiling. Stars are everywhere."

I didn't agree, but I didn't have a good argument. I'd already circled all the other trees, and the rest of the carvings had been faded and shallow. Not like this sharp, clear star. I ran my fingertips over the wood, feeling each line of the star. The wood was rough, and sandy bits stuck to my fingers. When I raised my hands to my mouth to blow off the wood dust, my skin smelled like a forest.

"It's the only new carving here," I said.

"Right," said Amelia. "But it could have been done by anybody. I don't mean to be rude, but you might be seeing what you want to see. You might want this too bad."

I wanted a lot of things.

"Maybe," I said.

"Is this what you want most of all?" she asked, eyes sharp and focused. "Is this what you would wish for if you could wish for anything? To find out about Plantagenet?"

"I don't know," I said. "I don't think so."

"Then what is it? And don't say coffee this time."

I frowned. Amelia could be a little repetitive sometimes. Frogs, frogs, frogs, frogs. Wishes, wishes, wishes.

"Why do you care?" I asked.

"Because I'm curious," she said, like it was obvious. "Why does anyone ask anything?"

That made me smile. Any annoyance sort of drifted away. Because, honestly, Amelia was possibly the most curious person I'd ever met.

"To be back home in Charleston, I guess," I said. "That would be my wish."

She studied me with her scientist face, narrowing her eyes and cocking her head. "No way," she said.

I started to argue with her, irritated that she'd ask for my wish and then tell me I'd named the wrong one. It's not like you could measure the truthfulness of wishes, like she could keep track of my facts and figures like she kept track of her frogs.

"Look," I said, "that was . . ."

She was already turning away, pointing at her mother, who was gesturing for us to come back to the car.

"Hey, I still haven't seen that cool wall at Trattoria Centrale," Amelia said. "Will you show it to me? Before we take you home?"

I could have argued with her about wishes. Or I could go get a tasty cup of coffee and enjoy showing a friend—a brand-new friend—my favorite place in town. I was prepared to let the wish thing slide.

By the time we got to Trattoria, I really had to pee. For the first time in I couldn't remember how long, I actually needed to go to the bathroom for a reason other than staring at the walls. I was in such a hurry that I didn't even look at the purple writing when I first came in. I mean, it had said the same thing for the last couple of weeks. Only when I was turning on the water to wash my hands did I notice that something was different.

I turned slowly, not quite believing what I'd seen from the corner of my eye.

There was more purple writing than there used to be.

There were the first couple of lines in purple, then my colored-in block letters finishing the verses. And then, where I'd stopped, more purple writing had been marked—heavily—over the other comments that had been on the wall. Now I read:

> *We are Plantagenet. We are chosen.*
> WE WILL NEVER GROW OLD.
> WE ARE PLANTAGENET.
> WE WALK NEXT TO YOU.
> BUT WE ARE NOT ONE OF YOU.
> WE ARE PLANTAGENET.
> OUR HOME IS IN THE STARS.
> *We are Plantagenet.*
> *You could be, too.*

I forgot about everything—Amelia, coffee, the soap on my hands, Gram and Mom expecting me home soon. I kept rereading one word over and over: *you*. This wasn't just a message. It was a message to me. An invitation.

The Plantagenets wanted to meet me.

Chapter 8

RSVP

Amelia and I sat in my room. Well, I sat. She stood by Gram's old sewing machine, pushing buttons and pulling levers. She'd lined up at least a dozen spools of threads and was trying to fit a bright red one onto the machine.

"This thing is so cool," she said. "Can you sew?"

"No," I said. "But Gram can make anything."

Amelia gave up on the thread. She took a step back and strained to reach her foot under the sewing table, pumping at the machine's pedal like she was keeping time to music. I thought about telling her you had to plug it in to make it work, but I was afraid she'd sew herself to the table.

"I can't believe you wanted to go to my house again," she said. "I love your room. Look at all this stuff!"

She swept her arm around, past the odds and ends of useless things Gram kept in my bedroom: an old treadmill, a tiny rocking chair Mom had as a kid, an iron birdcage, an old-fashioned hair dryer that looked like it would melt your brain, a recliner, an ironing board, high-heeled boots that Catwoman might wear, a deflated basketball.

I shrugged. I was used to Gram's junk.

"So how do I find them?" I asked.

Two days after I'd found the invitation scrawled on the wall, my giddiness had faded a little. Because meeting whoever was writing those messages was a lot more complicated than it sounded. First I had to find her/him/them/it. And I had no idea where to look.

Amelia shook her head, tossing black thread into the air. "You've got me. It's easier with frogs. You just need a net."

"Not helpful," I said. "You're the scientist. Be logical. Think of a plan."

"I dunno," said Amelia. "Maybe you should write her back."

"Write her what?"

"Your phone number? Tell them to give you a call. Them, her, whatever."

We'd spent two days trying to figure out what to call whomever was leaving the messages. I mean, the messages said "We are Plantagenet." Plural. But the handwriting was girlie, and it was all done by one person. It didn't make sense.

"Let's just stick with 'her' for now," I said. "And I am not leaving my number on a bathroom wall!"

Amelia tossed the black thread back on the sewing table and flopped onto my bed, her elbows landing next to my knees.

"Okay, now we're getting somewhere," she said. "This is better. We've narrowed it down. So you don't want to leave your phone number on the bathroom wall. What do you want to leave?"

That was one thing I liked about Amelia. She occasionally got distracted by spools of thread or Eastern spadefoots, but she had a way of simplifying things. She could take the hundreds of thoughts flitting through my head and pluck out the one I needed to focus on. And once she'd plucked out a thought, we could deal with it. Problems were easier to solve when you broke them down into smaller pieces.

So what did I want to tell the Plantagenets? If I left a message, what would it say?

"She needs to know I'm interested," I said. "That I want to meet her."

"Good," said Amelia. "That's part one. You accept her invitation."

I leaned back against my headboard.

"And she needs to know how to find me," I said. "She has to be able to reach me so that we can meet."

"She already knows," Amelia said. "If you answer her, she'll know she can reach you on the wall at Trattoria."

I nodded. "True."

So what did that leave? I thought of all the swoops and swirls of writing on the bathroom walls. I thought of all the messages—the bizarre ones, the funny ones, the sweet ones, the poetic ones.

"I need to impress her," I said. "I can't just say, 'Let's meet.' She needs to know that I'm worth meeting. If I'm boring, she might change her mind."

"Well, you're not boring."

"Thank you. But how do I prove it?"

We spent the next couple of afternoons coming up with messages that would prove I was not boring. The right message needed to be fairly short—I did have to fit it on a wall. And it needed to be attention grabbing. We took a stack of paper and a couple of markers and let our imaginations run loose. We'd jot down a message, discuss it, and either throw it in the trash or keep it in the *maybe* pile. We tried being funny, being clever, being intelligent, being flattering. Some of our first attempts were pretty good. Some were not. . . .

Knock Knock.
Who's there?
Plantagenet.
Seriously? I love Plantagenets!

To You Know Who—
I'd like to meet you.
I'd be an idiot not to want to.
I'll go anywhere.
As long as you're there.
Do you have blue eyes and silver hair?

Roses are red.
Plantagenets are chosen.
I would like to meet one.
At room temperature not frozen.

Thank you for the invitation.
It would be a nice situation
To join you at a restaurant or even a gas
station.

If we met, I think I would like you.

I like how you write and
Paint pictures with words and
How you keep secrets
I can keep secrets, too.

Then, like I was a lamp and someone had plugged in my cord, the right words just lit up inside me. I knew what I was going to write.

IF I COULD WISH UPON A STAR
I WOULD WISH TO MEET YOU,
PLANTAGENET.
WE COULD MEET IN THE SKY
AND CATCH A RIDE ON A COMET.
OR SPIN AROUND SATURN.
OR WE COULD HAVE COFFEE.

"Perfect," said Amelia, when I showed her the piece of paper. "I wouldn't change a thing."

I didn't want to waste another second. It had been four days since we'd first seen the message. I didn't want the Plantagenets to think I wasn't interested.

"You want to go down with me now and write it?" I asked Amelia.

"Sure."

I stuck a black marker in my jeans pocket, then I

folded up my paper and stuck it in my other pocket, just to make sure I would get the message right, word for word.

"I wonder how long it'll take for her to write me back?" I asked. "I wonder where she'll want to meet. I wonder how many of them will come with her. I wonder how many of them there are. I wonder if they'll have to vote on whether or not to let me into the group."

And for the first time in a while, I thought of a question about the Plantagenets that I hadn't considered.

"I wonder if they'll let you in, too?" I said to Amelia.

"I'd like to be," she said. "I'd really, really like to be a member of . . . whatever."

"I'd like that, too," I said. "That's it then. They have to let us both in."

"So I'll come with you when you meet them?" she asked.

She had nothing but excitement on her face. No nervousness at all. I felt sure aliens would love her.

"Definitely," I said as we stepped into the elevator.

That night, my fingers still remembering the satisfying feel of pressing my marker against the bathroom wall, I could hardly sleep. I was so sure I'd hear back soon, that the Plantagenets would be moved by my message and want to meet me as soon as possible.

I was wrong.

There was no answer on the wall the next day. But that night, downtown Birmingham lost power for six minutes. Some sort of surge in the system, the newspaper headline said. The next night, our lights blinked off at 9:00 p.m. and didn't come back on until nearly 9:30.

I couldn't help thinking back to what I'd read. Those classic signs of alien invasion—what were they? Something like lights in the sky, flying discs, and electrical disturbances. I wasn't sure what electrical disturbances were, but I thought power outages might count. Something was blacking out entire sections of downtown. That something must be pretty powerful.

There was a third night of flickering power, and a fourth night where the power was out all night long. Gram bought a pack of a dozen candles since they were cheaper than flashlights. Well, she bought new batteries for the one rusty flashlight we'd managed to find buried in the closet in my room. She said a little dark wouldn't hurt us, and there was no reason to make a fuss.

After a week of electricity problems—and a week of me not hearing from the Plantagenets—the newspapers and the teachers at school seemed to think there was a definite reason to make a fuss. I read headlines like "Serious Investigations Ahead for Power Company?" and "City Shudders to Stop with Repeated

Outages." And one day in class, while we were taking a spelling quiz, Mrs. Snellhawk was closing the door when she saw someone in the hallway. There were some words I couldn't hear, and then Mrs. Snellhawk said that there was bound to be more crime if the whole city stayed in the dark every night.

I heard high heels click toward our class. There was a woman's voice speaking softly.

"It's absurd that electricity is this unreliable in the twenty-first century," Mrs. Snellhawk said. She was whispering very loudly. Maybe some people were actually working on their spelling quiz, but I'd finished mine and had nothing to do but listen.

"There must be some ugly secret the city wants to hide," said the other teacher, whom I couldn't see. "Some flaw in the power company's technology. The entire power system might crash permanently. The power would just go out and never come back on. Ever. You wait and see. I'd buy up lots of bottled water if I were you."

Then the high heels clicked again, and as the other teacher moved, I saw long red hair swing past the door. Ah, it was Mrs. Leekdurst, the drama teacher. I thought she was overreacting a bit, but I supposed that was her job.

I felt Rachel tap me on the shoulder.

"Do you believe her?" she asked.

"Not really," I whispered. I was a much quieter whisperer than Mrs. Snellhawk.

"My grandfather thinks that the government is hiding secrets," she said. "He believes that we have spy gadgets disguised as mosquitoes, and the fake mosquitoes draw your blood and take it back to labs so the government has it on file."

I didn't have a good answer for that.

"That sounds almost cool," I said finally.

"Of course, my grandfather also calls me Erica sometimes," she whispered back.

"Who's Erica?"

"The neighbor's guinea pig."

Mrs. Snellhawk shushed us, so I had to swallow my laugh.

At home, Mom seemed almost excited about the whole power outage thing—she said it'd be good for us to stop watching television at night. She said we'd use it as an excuse to tell ghost stories and make up limericks and play board games by candlelight.

We didn't have real board games, though. We had LEGOs and Candyland and Hungry Hippo, which Gram had bought as surprises for us before we showed up here. And, I mean, I liked all of those things when

I was six years old, but the thrill had sort of worn off.

At least that's what I thought until Mom and I got to work on a five-foot LEGO tower complete with doorways and balconies. We sat crouched in the living room for hours on Friday night, candles lit. Gram watched from the sofa and eventually brought us some broccoli to use for trees and bushes—"You can't tell anything about a building without some landscaping," she said.

It turns out that if you cut the stalk of a piece of broccoli really evenly, you can make it stand up on a hardwood floor.

By ten p.m., Gram had kissed us good night and headed to bed. I heard her bedroom door click. I waited a few seconds before I said anything.

"I didn't see the landscaping thing coming," I whispered to Mom. "I would have thought she'd think it was a waste of food."

She laughed.

"Talk to her, Mario," she said. "She's not that bad. She and I have had our issues, but she can be fun. She raised me, didn't she?"

"I guess," I said. "Hey, you want to add a wall around the broccoli? Then it'd be more like a garden."

A few more quiet minutes passed. We each sorted through the remaining LEGOs to find the ones we needed.

"You have any singles?" Mom asked. "I'd really like a yellow."

"No yellows," I said, feeling around in the shadows under my legs. "But, oh, here's a red."

I started thinking about a drawbridge. I wasn't sure how to manage the moving parts. I was also pretty sure a piece of broccoli had worked its way into my pajama pants.

"I don't want to go to bed," said Mom. "I'm tired of being in bed."

"You do need your sleep."

She rolled her eyes at me. Even in the almost-dark, I could tell she had a LEGO balanced on each knee.

"But let's stay up anyway," I said, and her teeth flashed in the dark.

You know how when you sit in the dark, with just a tiny candle or beam of a flashlight flickering around the room, everything seems different? You can't see much, but suddenly you can hear everything better—the wind outside and the creak of the floors and the rustle of flannel pants. The same room that seems boring and familiar in the light suddenly seems full of possibilities when you're crouched around a tiny light, watching the shadows. It can be uncomfortable or scary, but it can also be thrilling. Like the top of a roller coaster, when you know you're about to get to the best part of the ride.

"It's exciting, isn't it?" Mom said, like she was reading my mind.

"What?"

"The dark. The candles. It makes you think you feel like things are different. Like there's something out there. In a good way."

"Yes," I said. "I know what you mean."

That was it exactly. The darkness made me feel like something was about to happen.

Still, I got no response from my message. Two weeks went by. I was beginning to feel desperate. Had the Plantagenets seen my response? Had they seen it and decided they didn't want to get to know me after all?

There was no way to know. Every morning I walked out the door, dragged myself to school, picked up my books, handed in my assignments, and did all the other hundreds of things I had to do to get me through the day, thinking of nothing but getting to Trattoria to check for any new writing on the wall. And every day I stepped into the bathroom and felt the disappointment hit me in the rib cage.

One morning, after the bell rang for changing classes, I heard my name as I was headed out the door. It was Rachel, holding out a small white rectangle.

"I don't know if you've got plans," she said, "but

I'm having a birthday party in a couple of weeks. The invitation's got my address and everything. It's no big deal—just a few people and some cake and stuff."

I took the envelope from her hand. It seemed like it should have felt heavier, seeing as how it held everything I'd hoped for in those first days of sitting lonely and quiet at my desk. Now it wasn't quite the invitation I'd been hoping for.

"Thanks," I said. "That sounds great."

"Sure," said Rachel, swinging her bag over her shoulder. "Hope you can come."

I opened the envelope as I walked to social studies, in the middle of lockers clanging, tennis shoes squeaking, high-pitched giggling from clumps of girls, people bumping against me as we all rounded corners and pushed through doorways. I unfolded the invitation, which was made of thick black paper and designed like a chalkboard, with the details of Rachel's party done in pastel colors like chalk. In pinks and purples and greens, chalky handwriting told me where to go and who to call.

I fingered the paper, which felt rough between my fingers, not smooth like a real chalkboard at all. All the background noise faded away. I looked at the palm of my hand, half expecting to see streak of colors. The chalk hadn't rubbed off, of course. At least, it hadn't rubbed off on my hands. But the invitation was all over my thoughts.

The next morning, exactly seventeen days after I'd written my message on the bathroom wall, I woke up early. A little before five a.m., actually. Early enough that it felt like every time I blinked, my eyes might just stay closed. But I dressed quickly—a little afraid I might put my shirt on inside out since I didn't want to turn on a lamp—and got my stuff together, including a little plastic bag I'd bought at the art store. I left a note for Gram, who would be up around six a.m., saying that I couldn't sleep and had left for school early. I made it into the hallway without the door even squeaking behind me.

From there it was easy. I'd thought it all through while I tossed and turned in bed the night before. The streets were mostly empty—a few workers from Dunkin' Donuts and McDonald's hustling down the sidewalk, a bus or two, the occasional car going by. But mostly I had the sidewalk to myself as night turned into day, grayer and cooler than the spring days had been lately. I could hear my own feet on the concrete, pounding a soft, fast rhythm as I walked. I wanted to get where I was going before the streets got any more crowded.

Across from Trattoria, there was an old brick storefront. There was a sign on the double glass doors saying the one-story building was going to be converted to a wine shop next year but there wasn't any sign of construction. The windows were covered in cardboard, and the doors were padlocked. There were cigarette butts along the window ledges, and spiderwebs hung from the edge of the roof.

Not a particularly impressive building. But at some point, someone had decided not to let it slide totally downhill. The white bricks were as gleaming as they must have been on the day the store opened. Sometime recently, they'd been cleaned or maybe repainted. But they made a giant white wall. Good as a chalkboard or a clean bathroom stall.

I opened my small bag and pulled out the box of chalk I'd bought. They weren't tiny little white pencils of chalk—these were huge round cylinders, the size of dynamite. I had a handful of colors that left a powdery rainbow on my palm. I looked both ways down the street—no one coming—and pulled out a blue the color of the sky.

I worked fast. When I was done, the letters were bigger around than my head. They took up the entire wall.

PLANTAGENET
I STILL WANT TO MEET YOU ANYWHERE
I'LL GO TO THE STARS
IF YOU NAME THE CONSTELLATION
PLEASE RSVP WITH A DESTINATION.

Around the words, I'd drawn a rectangle with little curlicues at the edges. It looked a little like a party invitation.

Definitely not boring, I thought.

Chapter 9

MY HEART'S DESIRE

I waited and waited some more. Plantagenets, whoever they were, didn't rush.

Mom was starting to move around more, and it made me nervous. She climbed up and down the stairs without me, saying she needed to get her strength back. She went for walks around the block and started cooking dinner for me and Gram. She was standing and smiling and joking around, and I kept expecting her to fall to the floor and collapse. *Poof.* She would be lying there on the floor, and all the smiling and cooking would have been like a dream. The tumors would be back.

So I was tense, waiting to wake up. Waiting for real life to start again. It's a terrible thing when you're in the middle of a beautiful dream, where you can fly and soar through the clouds and you're fast and light and it's all amazing, and then you wake up. And you can't fly after all. The disappointment makes you not even want to get out of bed.

Don't worry, Mom said. *Don't worry, don't worry, don't worry.* She and Gram said it over and over, like when someone gets a song stuck in their head and just keeps singing the same line until you think your head will explode.

One night, the power had been out for a couple of hours. The power company kept saying they didn't know what was causing the problems and that the issue would be fixed soon. But night after night, everything went black. We were starting to get used to it. Mom and I sat cross-legged on the floor, trying to roast marshmallows over a fat red candle. It was going pretty slowly.

"Let's go swimming next week," she said.

"Next week? That soon? It's still a little chilly."

"It won't be chilly at the indoor pool," she said, popping her barely tan marshmallow into her mouth. "Come on, I'm dying to get back in the water."

It wasn't the best choice of words.

"I don't know," I said.

"I thought you'd be glad that I'm back to normal," she said, running her hand through her hair, which was shiny and bouncy in the candlelight. Her face wasn't washed out and grayish anymore—her eyes were bright and her skin was smooth. She did look normal. She looked better than normal. She looked beautiful.

That was part of the problem. It would be so easy to believe she was okay. It would be easy to fall into the dream. And if I stopped waiting and watching, I wouldn't be prepared. I couldn't let my guard down.

"Come with me," she said. "Swim with me. I'll get some of those rings we used to throw to the bottom of the pool. You love diving down to the bottom."

I didn't think I could do it. It almost hurt to think about being in the water with her. Why was that? Why did the thought of something so good and normal hurt worse than thinking of her in a hospital bed again?

"Maybe," I told her, but I stood up and walked to the window. I needed a little space to think.

As I looked out over the city, I frowned. Lately, I'd seen one of two things out of my window: the usual city lights flashing at me from all over town, or the complete darkness of a blackout. Now I saw neither. Most of the city was black, all right. But off in the distance, I could see a silvery glow. It spread over the treetops and lightened the sky. I would have thought it was the airport, maybe, except it was coming from the wrong direction. And this light was too white, too bright to be runway lights. The glow was fuzzy and pretty, more like the lights from a circus or a fair. And it was the only light in the middle of the darkness, like someone had plugged in a night-light for the city.

"Mom, come look at this," I said.

She stood and came to the window, her hand resting on my shoulder. Part of me expected the glow to vanish as soon as I tried to show it to her. That's what would happen in a movie. But it didn't vanish.

"What in the world?" said my mom, pressing her cheek against the window to get as close as possible. "There's nothing but houses over there. I think that's over in Forest Park."

After a few minutes, the glow faded and then died out. The city darkened to black, with not even a glimmer of moon or stars in the cloudy sky.

"I wonder if anybody else saw that," mused Mom as she headed back to the candle and our bag of marshmallows.

We had our answer the next morning. For the first time in days or maybe weeks, the newspaper headlines didn't focus on the blackouts. Instead the front page read, "Unknown Lights Spark Curiosity of Downtown Residents." Rachel and her friends were all chattering about the lights as soon as I sat down—my guess was that even people who didn't see the lights were talking about them like they had. There were all sorts of theories—an explosion, a house fire, top-secret government experiments, and, of course, UFOs.

It was a relief to get to Amelia's house that afternoon. There'd been so much talk about the mysterious lights all day that I hadn't been able to sort through my own thoughts. Amelia's yard was a good place for thinking. We were surrounded by green—drooping leaves and winding vines everywhere, a jungle of trees and shrubbery and out-of-control flowers. It felt like a world away from Gram's condo and our school, like instead of taking a car, I should have had to row a boat downriver, past alligators and snakes, over waterfalls, and through caves. But I didn't. I just had to wait with Amelia for her mother to pick us up from school. It wasn't as adventurous as my imaginary boat trip, but it was a lot less sweaty.

We sat in the grass watching two frogs enjoy their exercise time. They had plenty of room to hop in their boxes, but Amelia thought it was good for them to broaden their horizons and have new experiences, so she liked to let them play in the yard.

I was watching Bertha, who was apparently not a frog at all but something called a Fowler's toad, bump against my right foot. Bertha seemed to think my foot was some insurmountable obstacle, like the Great Wall of China or the Grand Canyon.

"I wish you'd seen it," I said to Amelia, who'd only heard about the lights when she got to school. "The whole sky was glowing."

"Me too," she said. "As soon as I heard, I knew you'd think it was them."

In our conversations, "them" almost always meant the Plantagenets. The rest of the time, "them" usually meant frogs.

"What else could it be?" I asked. "We suddenly start having blackouts and strange lights . . . it has to be related to the messages."

"So . . . ," Amelia said, trying to act casual, "that means you do think we're talking about aliens?"

When she said it out loud, it sounded so silly. Geez, even when I said it in my head it sounded silly. The truth was, I wasn't sure it was aliens. Even in my most excited, optimistic moments, it was hard to convince myself we had a blue-eyed race of aliens running around the city messing with the power lines. But I was more and more convinced that whoever—whatever—the Plantagenets were, they had powers. Talents. Secrets. Every day that passed made me want to meet them more.

It was hard to put into words, and I decided to just change the subject.

"Where did you get these boxes anyway?" I asked Amelia.

"My dad built them, or, at least, he sawed the pieces," she said, prodding a frog named Alexander until it took a giant leap. "I helped him hammer and nail them together."

I watched Bertha try to navigate my leg. "I've never even seen your dad," I said. "I didn't know he lived with you."

"Course he does. He works nights—his shift is from four till midnight. He's never here when I get home from school. I haven't seen your dad, either. Where is he?"

Even if she hadn't just explained about her dad, I would have known by the way she asked the question that in her world, fathers were safe subjects. That she assumed fathers were kind and good and interested. And alive. It's not like she was the first person to ask the question. I'd figured out I could tell a lot about a person just by the tone of their voice when they asked. Sometimes, like with Amelia, there was no thought, no concern, like they were asking "What's your favorite color?" Those people usually had a really happy life with their dads, and they assumed you did, too.

Sometimes there was a little hesitation when people asked the question, a little pause between the words, a little fear that this might be an awkward subject. A lot of times those people had parents who were divorced, so they thought my dad just lived somewhere different than my mom. In my experience, people whose fathers had died never asked the question period.

I watched Amelia run one fingertip along Alexander's spine, assuming frogs had spines. I ran through my normal answers: *I haven't seen him for a while. I never really knew him. He doesn't live with us.* Usually any of those were enough to stop the questions.

I didn't speak, though. I didn't use any of my automatic answers. I just sat there.

"Olivia?" said Amelia, her hand paused a few inches above the frog.

Here's another thing that's good about bathroom walls: Sometimes you have stuff in your head that wants out. It's too big to be held inside, but you're nervous about what might happen if you let it out in front of people. No telling how it might look or sound once it's outside of your head. It's like the time I had a piece of vanilla birthday cake left over, and I stuck it in a Tupperware container in the refrigerator. When I opened it a while later, it didn't look anything like birthday cake. It was green and purple and bubbly, and the smell made me want to throw up. So what if a thought is like that? What if it grosses people out once you take the lid off?

You don't have to worry about that with a bathroom wall. You let out the thoughts in your head—who you love, what you want, just the fact that you exist—and there's no one around to watch you let them out. If anyone reacts to you, you're long gone before they do. You won't have to see sympathy or pity or awkwardness on anyone's face. You don't have to have a conversation. You just let it out, leave it there on the wall, and walk away.

It had been a long time since I stuck the thoughts of my dad on the back shelf of my head. The lid was on very tight, but, lately, I'd been thinking I wanted to take it off the shelf. It was heavy, and it took up a lot of room in there.

"Olivia!" said Amelia. She'd turned away from the frogs totally, and she looked like she was about to call 9-1-1. "What's going on? You okay?"

I was fine. I just couldn't talk. So I imagined the air in front of me as a large white wall, totally blank. I imagined my mouth as a pen and my voice as the ink.

"He died," I said. "My dad."

I didn't look at Amelia. I let the words write themselves on the wall.

"I don't remember him. He was home watching me, my mom says. When I was two. And he had something go wrong with his brain. A little explosion in a blood vessel. So he died in less than a second. *Poof. Gone.*"

I had a sudden thought of the power going out. Lights one second, then everything blinking into darkness. I wondered if that was what it had been like for my dad.

"I'm sorry," said Amelia.

"I didn't know him. So I can't miss him. Right? You can't miss someone you don't know, can you?"

"I think you can. Probably."

"Maybe. Maybe you can. I think about him sometimes. We lived in North Carolina then, and he's buried with his parents there, so I don't even have a grave to visit or anything. But Mom tells me stories. How he used to hold me up and sing to me like I was Simba in *The Lion King*. How he used to moonwalk when she got mad at him, just to crack her up. How he drank coffee all the time, and he sweetened it with maple syrup, not sugar. But they'd only known each other four years when he died, so I don't know if she knew him too much herself. You need lots of years, don't you? To really know someone?"

"You know me. I know you," said Amelia.

"If he'd been around when Mom got sick, he could have helped. He was strong, she says. He used to do push-ups before he went to bed. He could have lifted her into the shower and held her up when she got dressed and carried her down to the ambulance when it came that one time. I tried to, but I had to leave her on the stairs and go wait outside without her. Do you think she would have felt better if he was still around?"

Amelia had scooted closer to me, her foot just an inch or so away from mine. "You're not really listening to my answers, are you?" she said softly.

I kept writing on the wall with my voice.

"Sometimes I think it would have been better if he were here. If there were two of us to help her. But, still, he wouldn't have known her as well as I do. I've had a lot more years with her. I know she can't chew gum because she always forgets and swallows it, and she's allergic to Windex, and she always gets teary-eyed when she sees an old person in a wheelchair. For some reason."

I could have gone on for hours about Mom, all the little things about her that I knew. I could have written an entire book on her—*Mysteries of Mom*, and it would've had a thousand pages of facts.

"So I'm the one who should know when there's something wrong," I said to Amelia. "I'd be able to see it better than anybody. If she starts feeling bad again and doesn't want to admit it, I'm the one who can tell if she's out of breath or holding her side or sleeping more than she usually does. If I'm watching her, I could maybe stop it."

"Stop what?" asked Amelia.

I looked at her. It seemed so obvious.

"The sickness," I said. "The tumors. If I see it happening again and I get her to the doctors, she'll have a better chance of getting well. The earlier they catch things, the better the chance they can fix them. I read that."

"But she's well, isn't she?" said Amelia. "She's totally recovered now. It's not like she had a disease or anything. She had surgery, they took some stuff out, and now she's all better."

"That's what they say," I said. "But so what? Dad was perfectly healthy. No surgery, no nothing. And—*poof*—he was gone. That can happen. It could happen to Mom."

"That's it, isn't it?" asked Amelia.

"What?"

"That's what your wish is about. Your wish is that she's really well. That the tumors are gone."

I reached down and picked up Bertha, flinching when I first touched her skin, which was rough and bumpy like something out of an alien invasion movie. But she was also cool and dry and surprisingly delicate. She trembled in my hand, her heartbeat thumping against my fingers.

"That's not my wish," I said to Amelia. I stroked my thumb over Bertha's head, watching the pulse beat in her throat. "My wish is that Mom gets well forever. Forever and ever. That she's never sick again. She never gets old or weak. She just stays strong and happy and perfect, and nothing ever hurts her again. That's my wish."

Bertha blinked at me. It's very hard to read a frog's expression. Amelia's face, though, was easier to read, even before she spoke.

"Oh, Olivia," she said, her eyes on the ground. "I don't think you can get that wish."

"You didn't ask me if it *could* come true," I said. "You asked me what I wished for."

She didn't say anything after that—we both seemed to become totally fascinated by the frogs. Eventually we went back to talking about a spot on Bertha's back and a fire drill at school and whether a bump on my arm was a mosquito bite or poison ivy. I mostly stopped thinking about either one of my parents. Then I found a sheet of paper from Mom when I got home. She'd taped it to the door of my room. The paper was a letter typed on hospital stationery, and attached to it was a yellow sticky note.

"Mario," wrote my mother in blue pen, *"I had my doctor give me this note just for you. Am out now bungee jumping. Be back about 6:00 p.m. Kidding about the bungee jumping. Am really buying groceries."*

The typed note read:

Dear Olivia:
I'm Dr. Ingram—I met you while your mother was still in the hospital. She's asked me to write you this note, which she calls a permission slip. I promise you that your mother has recovered wonderfully from her operation. We removed the tumors, and she's healed perfectly. She is in excellent health now, and she can do everything she did before the surgery. She has recovered.
She asked me to repeat that at least once.

She has recovered. I give you permission to
take her swimming.

Best,
Kathleen Ingram

When Mom came home an hour later, she dropped an
armload of brown paper bags on the counter, then shot
me a look like, "Well? Was that enough for you?"

I tried to look amused. I mean, really, I have a
decent sense of humor. But I had a hard time meeting
her smile. She was practically sparkling over there in
the kitchen, so giddy to be feeling strong again that she
looked like she might leap onto the counter and do a
little dance with the grocery bags.

I sat there knowing I didn't feel happy or amused
or even relieved. Relief would have been a reasonable
thing to feel when your mother's doctor guarantees
you she's all better. No, as I was sitting there wondering why I didn't feel any of those things, I realized what
I did feel: afraid.

The doctor's note scared me, and I had no idea why.

"So we'll go out later this week, huh?" said Mom.
"To a pool?"

"Sure," I said, but I knew my voice didn't sound like I
was sure.

We unpacked groceries, and later I helped Gram make spaghetti for supper—lots of red peppers, just like I liked it. Mom sprinkled extra Parmesan on my plate, and Gram tried to show me how to eat spaghetti with a spoon and fork at the same time. I should have had a great time. And I tried. I tried to taste how delicious it all was. But my mouth didn't seem to be working right. I could hardly taste anything, I couldn't smile like Mom and Gram were smiling, and I could barely manage to speak to them.

I left half the spaghetti on my plate and asked to be excused. When Mom asked me if my stomach was bothering me, I said of course not. I said everything was so wonderful that I couldn't handle any more. She laughed and let me clear my plate.

My appetite didn't really come back that night.

It didn't come back the next morning, either, not even when Gram made pancakes.

By the end of school that day, I was getting concerned. I didn't know why the fact that Mom getting better made me feel so unsettled. But being unsettled was one thing—not enjoying food was a whole other thing. An unacceptable thing. I figured maybe a scone would jolt my stomach—or taste buds or whatever—back into action.

And, of course, on the first day where I hadn't been

obsessing about the Plantagenets once every five minutes, I finally heard from them. The chalk must have gotten their attention faster than boring old marker on a bathroom wall, because the answer to my chalk message was written on the bathroom door of Trattoria.

> Let's do meet,
> Though Saturn is a bit far.
> You know where my home is.
> Meet me there for coffee
> 6:00 p.m. this Thursday.

Chapter 10

A CUP OF TEA

The note kind of freaked me out at first—I mean, find a place not on this earth where I could buy coffee? My first thought was that NASA had set up a space station with a coffee bar. Then I thought about all the coffee shops I knew so well: Other than Trattoria, there was Urban Standard, Celestial Realm, La Reunion, Crestwood Coffee. I had a feeling I knew what Celestial Realm meant, but I thought I'd look it up to make sure. (When I was little, every time I asked her what a word meant, Mom drove me crazy by telling me to look it up in the dictionary. It had become habit.)

The dictionary told me this:

celestial: (adj.) Relating to the sky or heavens

realm: (n.) a community or territory

That seemed clear enough. But Celestial Realm

was too far to walk from the apartment, which meant we needed someone to drive us. I didn't want to ask too much of Olivia's mom since she'd already taken us to the high school, and Mom did keep pestering me to give Gram a chance. So I asked her for a ride. That got me a lecture about coffee not being good for young women. But it also got me and Amelia an invitation to dinner at Gram's favorite restaurant, Rojo.

That was more helpful than it sounds. Because Rojo happened to be next door to Celestial Realm. Apparently Gram felt like caffeine was less harmful on a full stomach.

So on Thursday night, Amelia and I sat across a table from Gram, devouring quesadillas and something called Hog Wings, which were like hot wings only they were made of pork. Very tasty.

Gram had handed us the kids' menu when we got there. "Ages eight and under," I'd read aloud. And she'd looked at me a little puzzled until I said, "And I'm eleven, remember? I usually order off the adult menu now."

I was a surprised she didn't expect me to entertain myself with crayons and a coloring book.

Anyway, we'd nearly finished our quesadillas—my appetite was back to its old reliable self—when Gram surprised me.

"So you two aren't really just interested in coffee, are you?" she said.

I took my time swallowing. Gram had a little bit of roasted pork on her cheek, and it seemed like a good time to mention it.

"You have something on your cheek," I said.

She swiped at it and kept watching me, not losing focus at all.

"What do you mean?" I tried again, kind of laughing that she'd asked a silly question.

"Why are you really going to Celestial Realm?"

"It sounds cool," I said.

"They have a mocha drink that's supposed to be amazing," said Amelia. That was true. And it was about as much help as I could expect from Amelia. Because, really, it's sort of understood that you don't lie to other people's parents, certainly not other people's grandmothers. If there was lying to be done, it had to be me.

"Uh-huh," said Gram. "Right. Now, what's the real reason? You're two smart girls. I can see your brains working. You're planning something. Don't try to distract me with pork this time. I can only have so much food on my face."

It occurred to me that sometimes I underestimated Gram.

"No reason," I said.

She just kept looking at me. Amelia just kept eating her quesadilla.

"It's nothing bad," I said.

She kept looking at me. Her hair was puffed like a gray cloud around her face, and her eyelashes were long and thick like Mom's. I let myself stare at her eyelashes for a little while.

"Here's the thing," I said, and it was maybe the first time I had talked to Gram like a real person and not like a very nice stranger who let us live with her. "There is a reason. It's nothing bad. It's not, like, meeting boys or anything. But it's a secret and I'd like to keep it a secret. If you don't mind."

I clenched and unclenched my fists. This, I thought, was the problem with having moved around her politely in the condo. With having not talked much. With having been so determined to act like this was not permanent and she was not permanent and that we didn't need to know each other. Now when I was desperate, I had no idea what she was thinking. What she would say. We looked at each other for a little while over the empty basket of chips and the cold queso, and then she smiled.

"Fair enough," she said, and she reached over and took my hand in hers. Her hands were warm and soft and for some reason made me think of biscuit dough.

"I'm not just a grandmother, you know. I'm an actual person. I've had secrets. I like secrets. I say give a girl a good friend"—she nodded at Amelia—"and a good exciting secret, and you've got everything you need."

"Really?" I said, leaning forward and accidentally setting my elbow in a puddle of cheese. "You say that?"

She winked at me.

"You can go to the coffee shop. I will stay here. I will not cramp your style. But you've got an hour before I'll come over there to make sure you're all right."

That seemed fair, really. So we finished our food, I kissed Gram on her poofy hair—which smelled sort of pleasantly of hair spray—and soon enough Amelia and I were strolling into Celestial Realm coffeehouse.

The minute we were inside, I forgot all about Gram. I forgot all about real life. I only wanted to think about whoever was waiting for us.

"I'm still not sure why she'd make the message into a riddle," I said, looking around the warm, softly lit room.

"And I keep telling you, she didn't want everyone in the city meeting her here at tonight," said Amelia. "Secret groups don't like to advertise their private meetings."

We paused as we looked around. I'd only been in Celestial Realm once before, and it was a little fancier than most coffee shops. Instead of tables and chairs, the shop was full of leather sofas and puffy chairs. Rugs of all colors lay across the floor, overlapping, and the teardrop-shaped lights hanging from the ceiling were rainbow-colored. The room looked soft and touchable, lit up with reds and purples and greens and blues all around.

"Now comes the real question," I whispered. "Who is it we're meeting?"

We scanned the room carefully. People were sprawled across four of the sofas and five of the chairs—a few students staring at books or computers, two couples obviously out on a date, an older man listening to headphones, a group of women about my mom's age laughing as they sipped at cups overflowing with whipped cream. None of them looked up at us, and none of them looked particularly mysterious. Definitely none of them looked like aliens.

None of it felt like I had expected. This was possibly the biggest night of my life, the night where everything would change forever. There was no telling what I might learn—the world might seem like a totally different place tomorrow. But the coffeehouse looked normal. The people looked normal. There was no sound track like in movies, where the music let you know something big was about to happen. All I could hear was the low buzz of conversation, the espresso machine whirring, and some guitar music playing over the speakers.

I had been expecting something more dramatic. Maybe dead silence when I walked into the room. Maybe spotting a group of people, probably dressed in black, possibly wearing sunglasses. People with mysterious expressions who talked in whispers, people who would give me a quick "come here" sign, scoot their chairs even closer together, and ask me to prove myself worthy of joining them. I didn't know that's what I expected until I looked around and saw nothing but totally unsuspicious, nonmysterious people.

"Maybe we should have included some sort of instructions in the message," said Amelia. "Like 'wear a green hat' or 'carry an umbrella.'"

I frowned. "Whoever they are, they won't have any idea who we are, either."

As I said that, I noticed someone new, someone not sitting in a comfy seat. Over against the wall, next to the shining glass coffee bar, stood a tall, white-haired woman. Silver-haired, even. She was staring right at us, sipping a hot cup of something and breathing in the steam. She smiled over her cup, and I wasn't sure if she was smiling at us or at the smell of her drink. Then she gave sort of a half wave, half salute. I looked behind me, wondering if she was acknowledging someone else.

When I looked back toward her, she'd turned away, facing a small hallway that led toward the back of the building. She looked over her shoulder directly at me and Amelia, then she started walking. She did not move like an old lady. She moved fast and easily.

"I think that's her," I said, taking off after her.

"Her?" Amelia pointed.

We had to rush to keep her in our sight. When we got to the end of the hallway, she turned a corner. We stepped into a small private dining room, the kind you could reserve for a birthday party. It had one long wooden table and eight chairs. The table was covered in platters—scones, muffins, tiny quiches, cut fruit. There was a tea pitcher and a French press of coffee, both steaming.

Distracted briefly by the food and the hidden room, I looked up into the eyes of the white-haired woman, who was standing perfectly still about two feet away from me. She had gray eyes, not cerulean.

"I suppose you are the young ladies with an interest in graffiti?" she said.

I nodded. She held out her hand, and when I took it in mine, she shook my hand with a strong, sure grip. Her nails were polished a very pale pink, which matched her silky blouse and skirt. Tiny pearls dangled from her ears.

"I am Cassandra Halley," she said.

"Nice to meet you," I said, not sure what else to say. I didn't know where to start. I studied her, hoping if I just looked more carefully, this might make more sense. This polite, well-dressed woman had been writing on bathroom walls?

"And it's very nice to meet you," she said. "I've been very curious who might walk through that door. I didn't expect there to be two of you. You're younger than I would have thought."

None of my possible responses seemed very polite: You are older than I expected. And more human. And pinker.

"How did you know it was me, Mrs. Halley?" I asked. She was an old lady—it's not like I could call her by her first name.

"You were looking for someone," she shrugged. "I've been here for half an hour, and no one else who walked through that door scanned the whole room like you did."

She gestured to the table.

"Won't you join me?" she said. "I wasn't sure what you liked to snack on, so I ordered a bit of everything."

We settled in at the table, and Amelia and I both

chose a scone and began picking them apart. We were stuffed full of quesadillas, but it was nice to have something to do with our hands.

"I'm sorry I took so long responding to your first request for a meeting," said Mrs. Halley. "I had gotten a bit busy. Time slipped away from me."

"What were you busy with?" asked Amelia, looking at Mrs. Halley like she was a rare Eastern spadefoot.

"A few things," said Mrs. Halley. "We'll get to that."

She sipped at her tea, and when she blew on it lightly, the smell of orange drifted over. "I suppose we should start with the high school, though. Plantagenet. That's back when I was Cassandra Mosely, before I met my husband, Lowell."

Something about that caught my attention. Cassandra Mosely. Who was now Cassandra Halley. So her husband had been named Lowell Halley. C.M. and L.H. The same initials I'd seen carved into the tree out at the old high school.

"Did you carve your initials into a tree recently?" I asked, setting down my scone altogether.

She stared for a moment and slowly nodded. "You found that, huh? You *are* observant. I did carve those. Just once. Lowell had been going out there every year or so and recarving it for the past few decades. He had a real fondness for leaving his mark on things."

"He sort of rubbed off on you, didn't he?" said Amelia.

She smiled. "You could say that."

I felt like I should just confirm a thing or two. Make sure we were on the same page. Maybe if I said things more directly this would stop feeling like a dream.

"You're the one who's been writing about Plantagenet on the walls, right?" I said.

She nodded.

"Are you the only one?" I asked.

"Of course," she said.

I waited for her to say more. She picked up a cinnamon scone and broke it in half. She tore off a small piece and popped it into her mouth. For a while we sat there, chewing. She chewed very neatly, I noticed, tearing off piece after tiny piece of her scone like I imagined princesses—or gerbils—did. She wiped her mouth with the corner of her napkin. I couldn't see that she'd spilled a single crumb. Meanwhile, I was pretty sure I'd dragged my hair into my coffee. Finally I couldn't stand it anymore.

"I'd love to know what the messages meant," I said.

There was still a chance that I hadn't been totally wrong. That this one woman was only the tip of the iceberg to something bigger and better.

"And I'd like to tell you," she said, crossing her legs. "I guess I was trying to decide where to begin."

"Maybe with the high school?" I suggested. She'd already started there, but we hadn't gotten very far.

"It's as good a place as any," she said. "Plantagenet is where I went to high school, of course. Class of 1949. But the story really starts with Lowell. I'd gone to school with him for two years before he first spoke to me. That's not even right—he didn't speak. He wrote to me. I should mention he was an artist. He did cartoons and sketches and all kinds of drawings, but he also had beautiful handwriting. He'd do banners for the football games and such—just markers on white paper, but they looked like they should have been hung in a museum."

So far this story was not living up to my expectations. The way Mrs. Halley told a story reminded me of how she ate a scone—it might have started out whole, but it got broken into pieces and scattered around. But I smiled politely and nodded encouragingly, hoping these bits and pieces would wind up making sense.

"I came to school one day in eleventh grade," she said, "and when I got to my homeroom, there was a big poster board taped right up on the wall that said, 'Cassie Mosely, will you go to East Lake Park with me this Friday?'"

"Did you think it was sweet?" asked Amelia, who

was apparently doing a better job than I was of going with the flow of the story.

Mrs. Halley rolled her eyes. "I thought it was tremendously embarrassing. Who asks a girl out with a sign in public like that? I ripped it down and threw it in the trash can. Teenage girls are not the nicest creatures. Try to remember that when some nice boy asks you out for the first time. Even if he's odd."

"You thought he was odd?" I asked.

She laughed—a very deep laugh to come from such a delicate-looking lady. It made me think of Santa Claus and jiggling bellies and pipes. I wondered if Mrs. Halley smoked a pipe.

"Oh, he was definitely odd," she said. "At any rate, he never even mentioned having asked me out. A few weeks went by, and he fell into step beside me in the hallway between classes. He asked me if he could walk me home. I didn't want to be rude—I at least had the decency to feel a little guilty about ripping up his sign. So I said I wouldn't mind. He walked me home, and for a while that was all. He'd show up next to me once a week or so, and he'd walk me home. Carry my books, tell me about whatever comic book he was working on—he was always coming up with new ideas—ask me about my day. It got to be comfortable enough."

"And then he carved your initials in the tree," I said, feeling like what I had hoped was a mystery story had turned out to be a love story. Love stories were much more boring than mysteries.

"Oh, that was much later," she said. "After the dance. After the dance, my dear, he carved our initials everywhere. Trees, fences, wet sidewalks, mud puddles, sandboxes. A whole lifetime of carving and scribbling."

She laughed again, and I expected to see little smoke rings coming out of her mouth. "There never was a man more interested in leaving a record of himself."

I felt like the story was falling into pieces again.

"No," continued Mrs. Halley, correcting herself. "It wasn't about leaving a record of himself. He wanted to leave a record of us. He wanted us—him and me, the fact that we loved each other—to be carved in every nook and cranny of the city. He told me one time that long after we were gone, he wanted the trees and the streets and rocks to scream out how he loved me. And that I loved him back."

She looked at us critically. "You two are too young to appreciate that, but, trust me, it's very romantic. I hope both of you find someone who loves you like that one day.

"He didn't stop once we got married either. Always carving initials or some such everywhere. Carving our names in the sidewalk outside our house. Handprints in the garden wall. That sort of thing."

She stopped.

"And then?" I asked.

She set her teacup very neatly back in its saucer. "And then he died. A year ago. Pancreatic cancer."

"I'm sorry," Amelia and I said at the same time.

"Thank you. I was very sorry, too. A bit lost really. Aimless. I didn't know how to fill up my days. I didn't like being alone in our house, so I just wandered around—shopping, walking, ordering coffee I never finished. Up and down streets, in and out of shops."

I nodded. When Mom had her operation, she had to spend two nights in the hospital, so it was just Gram and me in the condo. Those were the longest days and nights of my life. I couldn't stop thinking about what if Mom never came back, what if her bed stayed empty and her favorite coffee cup never got filled up and the shoes she'd left by the front door never got worn again. I couldn't stand seeing all her things that seemed so unimportant when she was there using them and holding them and wearing them, but that suddenly seemed so sad and empty when she was gone.

I could understand why Mrs. Halley wanted to get out of her house. I'd made every excuse I could to avoid the condo while Mom was in the hospital. That's when I discovered Trattoria Centrale, when I was desperate to find someplace to kill time. But after dark, when I had to come home, I'd curl up on Mom's bed and slip on her favorite Lucky Charms T-shirt, even though I normally made fun of her for wearing the raggedy thing. I'd slide under her sheets and drink decaf out of her coffee mug, even though I hated decaf, because she liked it. I wanted to taste what she'd tasted, feel what she'd felt.

Mrs. Halley lifted her teacup to her mouth, even though the cup was empty.

"You wrote on the walls because it reminded you of him, didn't you?" I said.

She smiled into her empty cup.

"It started out as a spur of the moment thing," she said. "Just a lark. Silliness. I happened to be in a restroom, and there was all sorts of boring business—bad words and names on the walls—and I fished through my purse, found a pen, and wrote the first thing that came to mind. And it felt good. It did make me feel close to him. Connected. So I kept doing it. I started carrying a purple pen with me all the time, and, when the mood struck, I'd jot down a phrase in the ladies' room."

She looked up, seeming self-conscious for the first time since we'd walked in.

"I'm not as creative as Lowell was, though. I just kept thinking about when we were first together. Our time at school. And for some reason the alma mater popped into my head."

"The alma mater?" I repeated.

"For Plantagenet High." She scrunched up her face for a moment, peered at the ceiling, and began to sing softly, slightly off-key.

> *We are Plantagenet.*
> *We are chosen, a unique breed,*
> *Forever striving upward and onward*
> *Always to succeed.*
> *Progress and truth*
> *Are our watchwords.*
> *Every wound we'll soothe.*
> *We walk next to you*
> *But are not one of you.*
> *Our works will be eternal*
> *We will never grow old.*
> *We are Plantagenet*
> *Brave and bold.*

She dabbed at her mouth awkwardly when she stopped singing.

"And so on and so forth," she said. "Forgive my

voice. It was a religious school. We were supposed to hold ourselves to a higher standard, I suppose."

"We are Plantagenet," I whispered to myself. We'd seen it on the high school sign. It made sense that it was part of the alma mater.

Amelia leaned forward. "So 'we will never grow old' means . . ."

"We'll live forever because of the deeds we do. The people we help."

"Oh," said Amelia. "That's disappointing."

I knew what she meant—that there was nothing supernatural about it. No eternal life or anything. But Mrs. Halley looked hurt.

"Pardon me?" she said. "I've always thought it was a beautiful idea."

I was still trying to concentrate on Mrs. Halley's song. Something wasn't quite right. She hadn't sung the most interesting part of the bathroom messages, the part that had gotten me the most interested.

"You didn't sing the part about 'Our home is in the stars,'" I said.

Mrs. Halley turned to me. "That part wasn't from the alma mater. That was just for me. A little saying of Lowell's. You're clever girls, apparently. Can you guess what he meant? That the two of us had a home in the stars?"

We looked as blank as the white wall behind us. No glimmer of any idea written on our faces.

She smoothed her already-straight skirt. "Does it help if I say in high school people called Lowell by his last name?

"Halley," I said. "Like Halley's comet?"

"Bingo."

"Okay," I said. "That explains him. Cassandra Mosely, though. I'm not sure."

"Everyone called me Cassie then," Mrs. Halley said. "Though Lowell didn't. He didn't think it was classy enough. He made up his own nickname, something more, oh, cosmic."

I stared down at my lap, which was covered in crumbs. Practically a constellation of crumbs.

"Cassiopeia," I said. "He called you Cassiopeia after the constellation. The one named after a beautiful queen."

"A beautiful vain queen," she corrected. "But I choose to think he was focused on the beautiful part when he came up with the nickname."

"That's it then," I said. "You were just remembering your husband when you wrote on the walls. None of it had anything to do with the blackouts, the glowing lights, all the headlines in the newspaper."

"The blackouts and glowing lights?" she repeated.

"I know, I know," I said. "It was just some glitch with the power company. I thought maybe it had something to do with Plantagenet."

She folded her napkin. "I'm sorry."

"No, I'm the one who was making up fantasies—" I began.

"I mean I'm sorry because I *am* the one who caused the blackouts," she said. "I was trying to make it all work. I didn't realize how much power I was using, and I wound up having to buy generators. I think the glowing lights were me, too. I didn't expect the news people to notice."

Amelia and I exchanged a glance.

"Notice what?" I asked.

"Oh, my dears, those scribbles were only the beginning," said Mrs. Halley. "They just got me to thinking. Remembering those early days with Lowell. How he loved to leave me messages. So I decided I would give him one last gift."

"Well . . ." said Amelia, but she didn't finish the sentence. I knew what she wanted to say, though.

"Um, so, I don't want to be rude . . ." I began. "But he's dead, right? I mean, passed away?"

"That's right. Eleven months ago."

"And you're going to send him a gift?"

"That's right."

Amelia and I looked at each other.

"So what do you say?" Mrs. Halley said. "Would you like to see it for yourself?"

Amelia and I looked at each other.

"We've got maybe forty-five minutes before my grandmother's going to come looking for us," I said.

Chapter 11

A HOME IN THE STARS

Even as Amelia and I climbed into Mrs. Halley's Cadillac, I wondered if we might be making a huge mistake. If Mrs. Halley might just be completely insane. That seemed harsh, even inside my own head. She definitely wasn't *completely* insane. But maybe a little nuts. In a nice way.

I'd been having thoughts of craziness ever since we left the restaurant. I mean, first, when she asked us to come back to her house with her, I thought: Of course we can't. She's a stranger. You can't get into a car with a stranger. It's stupid. It's how all those creepy television movies start. Then I thought, hey, the stranger is a lady in her eighties. And there are two of us. If she tried anything weird, we could surely outrun her.

But if she was crazy, all bets were off. Crazy people can have superhuman strength. I read that somewhere.

She'd said her house was only five minutes away. She'd said we could invite Gram to come with us. But I didn't want Gram to come—I wanted the secret, even if it would end up being a dumb secret, to be all mine and Amelia's.

So I sat in the front seat with Mrs. Halley, and I kept my hand on the door handle. Amelia was pressed against the door in the backseat.

"What got you interested in a few lines jotted in a bathroom wall?" asked Mrs. Halley, glancing in the rearview mirror as she pulled into traffic. "I've been leaving notes for months, and no one else has ever answered them."

"I saw one of your notes in Trattoria Centrale, then the next day I saw almost the same note at our school," I said. "I couldn't get it out of my head. It seemed like it had to mean something."

"You must be at Hargrove Academy," Mrs. Halley said. "The assistant principal is my cousin. We were meeting for lunch one day."

I was glad I had my hand on the door handle—we were speeding like crazy. Mrs. Halley took a turn and my head almost knocked against the window. I thought old ladies were supposed to drive slow.

Mrs. Halley sped through a yellow light, then she glanced over at me. "You said you thought it meant something. What did you think it meant?"

I rubbed my hand along the smooth leather of her front seat. I didn't know how to answer her. Important secrets? Magical powers? A whole exciting world hidden underneath the normal, everyday world?

"I don't know," I said. The turns and the speed were knocking the thoughts right out of me.

"I thought this might be about an invasion," I admitted.

"An invasion?"

"Like aliens."

There was a long pause, and I wondered if she was suddenly thinking that she shouldn't have invited strangers into her car. Because they could be crazy.

But then she laughed her deep, pipe-smoking laugh. "Oh. Well, I'm sorry to disappoint you. I'm not an alien. I'm not opposed to an occasional invasion, though. You could say Lowell invaded my nice quiet life sixty-odd years ago. Long hair, pants too big. Quiet most of the time, but then he'd let out a laugh like a horse. Like a horse having an asthma attack. Quite a disruption when he started following me around and asking to walk me home. He made it hard to think. And just when I was sure I didn't want anything to do with him, he snuck into my head. Started making me feel differently. Complicated everything. Which was good and bad. But you'd know all about that sort of thing, of course."

"No one's following me home from school," I said.

"No, not boys," she said. "You're too young for that. I hope. But finding my message on the bathroom wall was a bit of an invasion, now wasn't it? Turned your life upside down?"

"I suppose."

"It can be wonderful to have your life turned upside down."

I thought of Mom's pale still hands, her knees flopping out of the covers.

"I don't really like it turned upside down," I said.

Her eyes flashed to me.

"It can go either way. When I saw what Lowell did at the dance, it changed everything. And when Lowell died, it changed everything, too. That doesn't mean having your life shaken up is always a bad thing."

It felt like maybe I should steer her back to the important parts of her story. I didn't want to talk more about the ways your life can be turned upside down.

"You mentioned the dance before," I reminded her.

"Right. The dance," she said, slowing—thank goodness—at a stop sign. There was no one else on the street, I guess, because she just stopped the car completely while she answered me.

"I know I'm a little scatterbrained," she said, like she'd been reading my mind. "It's just that there are so many strings to the story, it's hard to knot them all together. It's all about Lowell, and *everything* in my life seems to include Lowell. So it's a lot of material to sort through."

I looked into her gray eyes—like rain clouds, I thought—and I felt every bit of impatience empty out of me. I thought about what it would be like if I was trying to tell someone the story of me and Mom. It wouldn't have a beginning or end, really. I'd probably have trouble making a tidy story myself.

"No problem," I said. "Really."

She reached down and patted my hand before she hit the gas.

"The dance is where the story really starts, I suppose," she said. "The dance and the supernova. There'd been a supernova my junior year in high school, and it was the first any of us had ever heard of. Do you know what a supernova is?"

"It's when a star explodes, and most of its mass

shoots out into space," I said. "It gets very bright."

"Oh," said Mrs. Halley, eyebrows shooting up. "Yes. Very impressive."

"Olivia knows everything," announced Amelia "She should be on a game show."

"Clearly," said Mrs. Halley. Her eyebrows still hadn't come back down.

"At any rate," she said, "since there'd been so much interest in the sky that year, the theme of our prom was 'Going Supernova.' It was supposed to be all about the stars and constellations and such. Lowell had signed up to be on the committee, in charge of decorations. And he'd asked me to be his date months before the actual dance."

"So you'd been looking forward to it?" asked Amelia.

"Oh, yes. But because I was excited about another boy. I'd turned down Lowell at least three times. With no sympathy whatsoever. I still thought he was an oddball. The night before the prom, he told me that he'd arranged something special for me at the prom. That when I came to the dance, I should be sure to look up."

"Look up and what?" Amelia asked.

"That's what I thought," said Mrs. Halley. "But that's all he said. So I showed up in the gymnasium with my date, a lily corsage pinned to my dress, all enraptured by my date's dimples and how much he seemed to know about football—the boy had shoulders as wide as a Buick. When we walked through the doorway, it occurred to me to look up. And then I saw what Lowell had done. There were lights everywhere. All over the ceiling. I cannot express to you how many lights. It positively glowed in there.

"But it wasn't so much the number of lights—it was the pictures the lights made. He'd copied the real-life constellations: the Big Dipper and the Little Dipper, Orion, all the zodiac signs."

"And Cassiopeia?" I guessed.

"And Cassiopeia," she said. "Which happened to be right next to a very large, very bright Halley's Comet. Those two were the centerpiece of the whole prom sky. Not astronomically correct, but very sweet."

She shook her head and shrugged.

I could feel the car slowing down.

"All of a sudden my date's dimples weren't quite as irresistible," she said.

As she spoke, Mrs. Halley pulled into a driveway. The only light was a streetlight by the driveway, but I could make out a long, one-story brick house. The front yard was wide and full of what I guessed might be azalea bushes.

"Here we are," she said. "Home sweet home."

We piled out of the car, and as soon as she slammed her door, Mrs. Halley started walking. I might call it trotting—we had to jog to keep up. But we didn't head toward the front door; instead, she cut through the thick grass and made her way to the side of the house.

"We're not going inside?" I asked.

"What I want to show you is in the back," she said.

She led us around a side pathway, and we crossed through a tall, ornate iron gate that reminded me a little of my old cemetery in Charleston. The sun was setting, and the whole backyard was in shadows, but I could tell the place was huge, grass stretching out forever. I really hoped she didn't have any dead bodies back there.

As we rounded a corner, passing under a couple of ancient-looking trees, I saw a large building along the edge of the yard. It was about the size of a small house, but it was made entirely of glass. The setting sun reflected off it, and it was blinding to look straight at it.

"It's Lowell's greenhouse," Mrs. Halley said. "He never was too good with plants, frankly, but the greenhouse was here when we bought the place. He was always trying to do roses or orchids or some such thing. They never really worked, and I've let everything in there fall apart. But we're not coming in here for the greenery."

"What are we coming for?" Amelia asked.

"You'll see in just a bit," Mrs. Halley said. "It'll be more fun if it's a surprise."

Once we got to the greenhouse, she unhooked a latch and opened the door for us. I stepped in, and it felt like summer. It was a good thing we weren't coming for the greenery, because nothing was green. There were beds of dirt with dried-up branches and leaves drooping over the edges. Turned-over flowerpots. Crickets and cockroaches belly-up on the cement. There was a smell that reminded me of when I tried to grow roots on a potato for a school project, but the potato did nothing but turn black and collapse.

The potato smell was when the disappointment really hit. Back in Celestial Realm, I'd realized I'd been wrong about the Plantagenet messages. But only standing in the middle of the greenhouse did I really feel it. Everything I'd hoped for had been ridiculous. It's not like I'd really believed in aliens. But I'd wanted to believe that there was something out there, something hidden and spectacular and powerful, that would make more sense than real life did. I wanted to know that in the middle of dealing with tumors and gravestones and new schools, there was something bigger and brighter than all of it.

I hadn't found any of that. I'd found a sad, sort of

charming old woman who missed her husband. And that was it. The end. No magic, no hidden world, no mysteries revealed. All my hoping and wishing had led me here to a dirty, dusty greenhouse that was full of junk and smelled like rotten vegetables.

"I know it doesn't look like much," Mrs. Halley said, pulling the door behind her. "For some reason I started coming out here at night after Lowell died. All the dust and dark and gloom suited me. It looked like I felt. Then after a while I thought I might change things."

It didn't look like she'd changed anything to me. The glass panes were so filthy I could barely see the sky. I could barely see anything above me, really, other than a few spiderwebs in the corners that looked like Halloween decorations.

Mrs. Halley pointed toward a wooden bench that looked relatively clean.

"Have a seat," she said, stepping over to a cabinet that held a fan, a couple of extension cords, and other metal odds and ends.

"Maybe we'll just go on and . . ." I started to say, looking at the floor.

Then Mrs. Halley plugged in an electrical cord, and the entire ceiling exploded in white light. At least it seemed like an explosion at first—it was like someone had set off a giant fireworks display, except that these lights didn't fade away. They seemed to get brighter and more intense, more complicated. Once my eyes adjusted, I could make out loops and swirls of lights draped all over the glass ceiling of the greenhouse. And the more I stared, the more the lights took shape. They weren't just strings of lights—they were pictures. Stories. Stories jammed close together and overlapping like the writing on the wall of Trattoria Centrale.

It was like nothing I'd ever seen.

There was the sparkling white outline of waves with a whale leaping toward a white sun. There were two people waltzing, the woman in a long skirt that nearly touched a fireplace flickering with flames. There was a fish caught on a line, but the man holding the fishing pole was about to topple from the narrow tip of a boat. A baby's foot grazed the side of the fish as the baby's hand reached for a ball. A dog jumped over the baby. Two children slid down a hill on a sled. All these things were side by side, top to bottom, filling every inch of the ceiling. All of it was drawn in the white bright lights, shifting and flashing with the dark blue evening sky in the background.

"I couldn't do it all myself," Mrs. Halley said, looking

toward the sky. "I wish I could have. But I had to get the boy who mows the lawn to come over with a couple of his friends. I can't climb ladders like I used to."

"You designed it all?" I asked.

"Oh, yes. I drew it all out on paper. Where the lights should go. What these constellations should look like. 'Our home is in the stars,' you know," Mrs. Halley quoted, looking up toward the night sky. "I hope Lowell's home is up there now. I hope he can see this from wherever he is."

I kept staring—it was impossible to look away.

"What's that?" I asked Mrs. Halley. I pointed at a man standing on what seemed to be a table, with a ratlike something standing nearby.

"That's Lowell running away from the neighbor's dachshund," said Mrs. Halley. "That dog chased him around the house until he jumped on the dining table. I've never laughed harder in my life."

She must have noticed the look on my face.

"Everything up there is a story," she said. "From our life. My own version of constellations. I want him to know I remember."

"What's that one?" asked Amelia, who hadn't once looked away from the lights overhead.

"That one?" said Mrs. Halley, pointing. "That's my

niece climbing a tree. We joked that she had squirrel genes."

"And that?" I asked, noticing what looked like a castle.

It turned out it was a castle, a famous one in Spain where the Halleys went for their honeymoon. We kept asking questions, and she kept answering us, telling the story behind each picture. I don't know for how long. You can't measure time when you're in the middle of a universe. Hours and minutes don't work the same.

"Do you like it?" Mrs. Halley asked finally.

I turned to her and her face was reflecting the bright light like a moon. Her eyes held a thousand stars in them. The lights—stars or constellations or whatever—weren't just above us. They were shining down on us, sinking into our skin. Star tans, I thought. We're getting star tans. Right then I could believe that when we left this greenhouse, our skin would still glitter like the night sky.

"Oh, yes, I like it," I answered. "And I know your husband likes it wherever he is. It's the most amazing gift I've ever seen."

"It's not just for him," she said. "It was for me, too. It's a nice reminder."

"Of him?" I asked.

"Yes. But it's not like I could forget him. No, what I

needed reminding of was that if I didn't like my view, I needed to look harder. I could stare up at an empty sky, or I could look hard enough to find some stars."

I breathed in the smell of decaying potatoes, and all of a sudden it didn't seem so bad. I thought that instead of potatoes, I got a whiff of dried roses and the perfume of gardenias. I stared up at the web of lights over my head, and I could see the black sky beyond them. I thought I understood what Mrs. Halley was saying. You could look up and see an empty black sky if you wanted—you could think of the darkness as a huge, frightening thing. Or you could look for stars. You could even make stars.

That was the trick. Something as big as a sky—or a bad sickness or a dead father—could seem overpowering. It could seem like it would crush you. But you couldn't let it. You had to find the magic in things. It didn't have to be aliens or mysterious societies. The magic could be in anything. It could be anywhere. Magic could be lighting up greenhouses, or hopping like a frog across Amelia's backyard, or flickering like a candle while you built a LEGO tower with your totally healthy mother. Maybe all you had to do was look.

Amelia and I could only stay a few minutes in the greenhouse that night. We promised Mrs. Halley a longer visit next time. But for just a little while—before we sped back to Celestial Realm to meet Gram—we pulled together chairs and tilted our heads back. We propped our feet on the edges of an empty flower bed, and we stared up at the lights.

Chapter 12

AFTER THE LIGHTS WENT OUT

A couple of days later, I went to Rachel's birthday party. Rachel opened the door and said hello, but then her mother called her from the kitchen, so she waved me toward another room and said to help myself to snacks. She disappeared through an open door and left me to walk into the den alone. My tennis shoes made little squeaks on the floor, and I spent those first few steps wishing Amelia had been invited—it would have been nice to have her next to me. Without her I was nervous. Were my shoes too loud? Was the snow globe a stupid present? Would I freeze up? Had this whole party been a terrible mistake?

I barely looked around the den when I got there. There were balloons. There were a table of snacks and a table of presents, plus a few girls sitting on the sofa and another group standing by a fireplace. I smiled at no one in particular and took my time setting my birthday present on the table with the other presents. I fixed the bow. I straightened the tablecloth. Out of the corner of my eye, I could recognize a couple of girls from homeroom, but none of them were looking at me.

I decided to go pour some lemonade. That would eat up a few minutes.

But then, on my way to the ice bucket, I had another thought. I didn't really have to find ways to fill the time. I didn't have to wait for someone to talk to me. If I'd just turn around and walk up to those girls, I could be my old, unfrozen self. Or maybe a whole new self. No one was stopping me.

I did turn around. I took a few steps and then I was there by the fireplace, and all I did was say hello.

"Hey, Olivia," said a girl from homeroom. Her name was Tearra. "Do you know everybody?"

I said I didn't and they told me their names, and someone asked me where I was from, and someone else said her sister went to college in Charleston. And, after that, the words came easy.

A couple of hours later, I sat in the dark with six other girls, my fingers still a little sticky from chocolate cake, and watched a movie about a boy who traveled around the world in a giant balloon. The balloon floated across the screen, and, next to me, Rachel's eyes reflected tiny squares of light as she looked at the television.

"Did you see the one about the three kids who climbed Mount Everest?" she whispered to me.

"Nuh-uh," I whispered back. "But in real life the youngest person to reach the top of it was a thirteen-year-old guy. He was trying to climb the highest mountains on every continent."

"Sweet," she said.

I didn't feel frozen at all.

A shout from the TV hushed us, and we let ourselves fall back into the movie. We looked down on the earth from the giant balloon, miniature trees and lakes and hills as far as we could see. Several pairs of feet partially blocked my view since all of us were sprawled over the couch and the chairs and the floors. We'd painted toenails earlier, so I watched the blue and yellow balloon sail over a sea of pink and purple toenails.

To sit there with those girls, not the least bit nervous about whether or not I was saying the right thing, was magic. I could feel it inside me, filling me up like I was a giant balloon.

The next day, I went swimming with my mother. I watched her dive, slick as a dolphin, into the deep end, and when she swam up and broke the surface, she was laughing. She waved at me, dipped her head back in the water and made a face like it was so wonderful, so perfect that I'd be an idiot not to join her.

So I did. I took small measured steps toward her— no running at the pool—and I walked right past the ladder. When I got to the edge of the deep end, I took a step back, grinned at her, and threw myself up in the air. I curled and tucked and slammed into the water with the best cannonball I'd ever done. I sank to the bottom, pushed off the cement, and knifed through the water into the air.

"You drenched me!" squealed Mom.

"You were already wet."

"Oh, really? That's your argument?" She took a stroke toward me, and I took a stroke back. She had a sharklike look in her eyes.

"Let's see who gets who wet," she said, leaping for me.

She dunked me under, and as soon as I got loose, sputtering, I lunged for her. We were both spitting water and shrieking, and the water in my eyes made everything spin like I was on a merry-go-round.

"Too slow!" said Mom in my ear.

Her skin was warm and slick, and she was hard to get a grip on. She twisted away from me, and as she looked back over her shoulder, it occurred to me that she might swim forever. She was a mysterious and unexplained thing herself. I didn't need to protect her. I needed to enjoy her.

I took a deep breath, wiped the water from my eyes, and leaped after her.